Sparrowhawk

a Victorian ghost story

Paul Finch

First Published in 2010 by
Pendragon Press
Po Box 12, Maesteg, Mid Glamorgan
South Wales, CF34 0XG, UK

ISBN 978 1 906864 25 5

Typeset by Christopher Teague

Printed and Bound in Wales by
MWL Digital Print, Pontypool

www.pendragonpress.net

Sparrowhawk

Neither day nor night existed in the Fleet Prison for Debtors. Even in the long, deep yards, the sun and moon seldom shone. All light there was grey and dim, all sounds faint, muffled. Supposedly built for exercise and association, these yards were in fact confined spaces of dense shadow and aching silence. A similar gloom pervaded inside the building – deadening the senses, stifling the breath. In the Fleet, time itself was an abstract concept.

Miss Evangeline went there unwillingly. Debt was not a condition that would ever apply to her, but she derived no pleasure from the trials and tribulations of others. It was a wet and very cold November day when her carriage pulled up on the prison forecourt. She bade her coachman come back in half an hour, then produced her letters of introduction and gazed up at the awesome structure. It was an architectural monstrosity, somewhere between a castle and a warehouse. Its brick walls were black with soot and streaked white and grey by the flocks of dirty pigeons that roosted in its high, rotted gables. The few windows visible were tiny apertures, heavily barred.

A tall, brutal-looking turnkey passed her through the first gate into a small entry passage, where her papers were examined. To the left was the door to the warden's house. Miss Evangeline

1

wondered if it might be politick to call there first and explain herself, but then she had second thoughts. Why spoil that sanguine official's day? In this small domain the warden was king; it seemed a pity to remind him there were infinitely greater powers. She took her papers back, and a second turnkey admitted her through another gate. This second fellow, even burlier and more brutish than the first, was entranced. Miss Evangeline was exceedingly pretty, with violet eyes, rosebud lips, a pert, pixie nose and honey-blonde hair fashioned in ringlets. Her pert figure was gorgeously clad in a pink bustled dress, high bonnet and cashmere shawl.

The turnkey became ingratiating and asked if she would like to come into their "lodge" for some tea, and maybe see "the portrait room", where they "sized up the new arrivals". Miss Evangeline politely declined, and so was shown through into the prison proper.

Here, a stench assailed her like offal or faeces. The transformation from broad daylight to dungeon-like darkness was briefly blinding. It was a warren of damp passages and dingy rooms, and already she was among prisoners. At first they were shades: spectral figures drifting aimlessly, heads bowed. But as her eyes attuned, she was able to see them for the miserable, broken wretches they were. Most wore the clothing of gentlefolk gone to seed, though there were also paupers' rags on view, bare feet, lengths of shin and wrist grown long past the extent of the childhood garb that clad them. Faces were haggard and pale, hair long and ratty, eyes red-rimmed. When Miss Evangeline asked an old man where she could find John Sparrowhawk, she was ignored. When she persisted, the man nodded at a stone stair dropping into darkness.

"Down there?" she enquired.

"The Fair, miss," the man said.

"The Fair?"

"Bartholomew Fair," he added, as if this explained everything.

Miss Evangeline nodded an understanding she didn't feel, and

descended the stair to a tunnel where water dripped incessantly and strips of dust-thick cobweb hung like pieces of tattered brocade. She glanced through one door after another. Weak candle-flames revealed mouldy straw, black ceilings, walls so damp they'd turned green. When she reached the end room and found the person she was looking for, it was no surprise that she barely recognised him; if anything could change a man it was this hellish place. He was a slumped in a corner, for there were no benches or chairs. A face once tanned and neatly chiselled was now pale and drawn, dark with unshaved stubble, framed on either side by a mop of lank hair hanging almost to his shoulders. Eyes formerly hard as jewels had sunk into their sockets. The one-time strong physique, so often resplendent in dress-uniform, was now skeletal and attired in a threadbare shirt and trousers caked with grime.

The first the prisoner knew of his visitor was her scent – a faint floral odour, rose and jasmine perhaps. He stared up at her, bleakly.

If it seemed strange to him that so decorous a lady, clearly one of status and breeding, had arrived unannounced in this place of the forgotten, he didn't show it. Perhaps his capacity to feel surprise had been crushed out of him, along with his bearing and his manners – and his ability to suffer cold. The temperature was almost sub-zero, yet though his skin was pale as ash and there was barely a scrap of meat on his bones, he didn't even shiver. She realised that his relatively brief incarceration – brief compared to some fellow prisoners, that was – had hardened him to a frightening degree. Though of course the North West Frontier might also have played its part.

"They call this part of the prison 'Bartholomew Fair'," Miss Evangeline said.

"I know." The prisoner got awkwardly to his feet. "I imagine it's a kind of irony."

"Bartholomew Fair was notorious for its lascivious pleasures." She looked him over properly now that he was standing. "Have

you enjoyed much lascivious pleasure, Captain Sparrowhawk?"

"Not of late," he said. "Are you offering some?"

She didn't dignify that comment with a reply, but surveyed the room. In one corner, a cracked pot served as a latrine. A black beetle clambered out of it.

"Who are you?" he asked.

"You may call me 'Miss Evangeline'."

"I may call you something else, miss, if you don't cease toying with me."

She tut-tutted. "How ungentlemanly that would be. If you don't mind your tongue, sir, I might deign to believe everything they say about you."

"Were you a friend of my wife's?"

"My relationship with your wife is of no consequence."

"So you were?"

"I didn't say that."

"Are you another who blames me for her death?"

She raised a finely-drawn eyebrow. "Did you kill her?"

"Of course not."

"So why should I?"

He seemed confused. "Not everyone I know has that clarity of vision. So why *are* you here?"

"I have a proposal for you, captain."

"Ahhh … the army sent you."

Miss Evangeline touched a handkerchief to her nose. The smell of sweat and dirt seemed to get worse the longer she spent in this necropolis. "The army?"

"As a honeyed lure."

"I don't understand."

He chuckled. "Don't tell me … Lord Ellenborough insists that we retake Kabul, and he needs all the suicidal subalterns he can get his hands on?"

Miss Evangeline shook her head. "The Afghan War is over. The British recaptured Kabul, and General Pollock's 'Army of Retribution' laid waste to the Afghan towns and villages on a

4

wide scale, massacring the tribesmen, both friends and enemies alike, as a stern lesson. The army then withdrew to India, wreaking more slaughter on the way and losing countless more of its own."

"Bravo to General Pollock. The Duke of Wellington always said the greater problem with Afghanistan was not getting into it, but getting out of it." Sparrowhawk shrugged. "It makes no difference, miss. If your paymasters think I'm going to return to the Colours after kicking my heels for half a year in here …"

"I'm not trying to recruit you back to the Colours, though I suppose my proposition carries a certain risk."

"Why does that not surprise me?"

"We made a study of your military career before coming to you, captain. It seems that your reconnaissance skills as a scout and mapper impressed General Elphinstone no end."

If the average man on the street heard a lady talk thus, it would have been shocking and baffling to him. But Sparrowhawk had been around army wives all his adult life, and his conviction grew about who had sent this handsome messenger.

"You were highly valued by all your comrades," she added.

"But not so much that any of my brother officers would throw me a credit line when I most needed it."

"Ah, well," she sighed, "that is the way of the world. Fall foul of Soho's gaming tables, and one is apt to lose friends as quickly as one loses one's money."

"Indeed?" Sparrowhawk said. "Well tell whoever sent you here that it's too late to buy me now. I owed only two-hundred pounds, yet not a single one of my former comrades came to visit me, or even sent anyone until this moment. And this, I learn, is because they *want* something."

"You're quite mistaken to think that this is an army matter,"

"So why do you keep using my military title? I resigned my commission months ago."

"I thought it might flatter you."

He chuckled humourlessly. "What a miscalculation."

"Yes, I fear so," she said, sounding sad. "Perhaps you aren't the man for us after all!" She moved to the door of the cell but, before leaving, added: "Do you want to spend the rest of your life in here? Because that's what it looks like. You've no income, no family ..."

"No friends."

"Captain ... the party I represent is offering to pay your debt, and all the interest you've accumulated on it. Not make you a loan, mark you, but pay it off in full."

Sparrowhawk leaned against a shelf, where his single stub of candle burned. "I served king and country for seventeen years, miss, and this is how they reward me. I don't want another piece of *that* cake, thank you very much."

"The choice is yours, though I'm surprised. I hear you once tried to escape."

"Two months after I was first incarcerated ... when I finally realised nobody was even reading my letters, let alone planning to reply to them. I made it onto the roof, but the turnkeys caught me. They beat me black and blue and threw me in the strong-room."

"You spent several days in irons, I believe?"

"It was more like several weeks."

"Not a pleasant way to pass your time. A pity if it had to happen again."

And she took her leave.

Sparrowhawk was left staring at an empty doorway, wondering if he'd imagined her final comment – hoping against hope that it had been a mere figure of speech, not an implied threat. Could he bear to be put back in irons, to be left in pitch-darkness, to be closed in a den so deep and foul that the rats were bold enough to nibble his toes even while he was awake? He had no intention of serving his country again; on that he was final. He had no country, anyway. As far as he was concerned his life was over, even if he was only thirty-four.

Yet for all that bravado, Sparrowhawk still couldn't lift himself from the mire of self-pity. During his months of imprisonment, he'd tried not to be resentful. He'd exercised every ounce of will he had to tell himself that this was nobody's fault but his own, that he had been frivolous, that he'd gambled with foolish extravagance. But then another voice – booming in his ear like cannon-fire – reminded him that he'd played and squandered no more than countless other young gentlemen newly released from war. Of course, unlike his fellow rakes and ne'er-do-wells, Sparrowhawk had had no-one to bail him out. Not that this was the real issue. The real issue was should he even be here? Was it right that a man honoured for gallantry in countless battles on the Sub-Continent, and wounded on the retreat to Jellalabad, should be locked away in this dismal place and forgotten? On the day of his arrest, he'd asked them this and they'd only sneered, calling him "a legend in his own mind". He'd fought with the bailiffs, blacking both the tipstaff's eyes, and they'd threatened to use that against him, saying that if he didn't come quietly they'd summon the peelers and he'd face a criminal charge.

He walked to the door and peered along the passage. It was empty. Miss Evangeline had already ascended to the upper levels. Even now, the turnkey on the front gate would be turning the lock for her. With a curse, Sparrowhawk hurried in pursuit. From the top of the stair, Miss Evangeline was visible at the far end of the next passage. Her bright, fashionable clothes stood out in that place where 'colour' was a meaningless term.

"Miss!" Sparrowhawk shouted. If she heard, she didn't look round. The gate was closing on her back when he reached it. "Miss, wait!"

Miss Evangeline glanced through the bars.

"What is this proposition you offer?" he asked.

She eyed him dubiously. "You're not quite the man I expected, captain. Are you sure you're fit for duty?"

"I thought you said there was no soldiering involved?"

"I didn't say that. I said I would not be asking you to rejoin the army."

Sparrowhawk clutched at the bars. "Why are you playing games again? Are you here just to torment me?"

"This is no game, captain, I assure you. I need to know – and mind you tell me the truth now – are you sure you wish to work for us. It will be very dangerous."

"Dangerous?" He laughed, and sniffed at the tainted air. "You smell that? … it's the River Fleet. It runs directly below us. If you think it stinks now, wait 'til high summer. In fact, summer is when this place is at its best. It swarms with vermin, the air's thick with bluebottles. We have outbreaks of cholera, jail fever. Every whore in this place is riddled with pox, but a man has needs, doesn't he?"

She didn't flinch at the ugly notion.

He continued: "We abound with blaggards. Every fellow robs another if he can. Many are taken out of here dead, and there is little or no investigation as to the cause. So don't advise me about danger, please."

She pursed her lips, before saying: "I can have you out of here in the next couple of days. In the mean time, is there anything you need?"

"A couple of pounds wouldn't go amiss."

"Not starting where we left off, captain?"

"My chummage has gone up this month."

"Chummage?"

"It's what we debtors have to pay for the privilege of being here." He gave a wry smile. "Believe it or not, we have to pay for the right to lodge. Then of course there's food and water, candles and coal … which also cost, and at a mark-up. The turnkeys do very nicely, let me tell you."

For the first time, Miss Evangeline looked shocked. Sparrowhawk knew what she'd be thinking: that such a thing wouldn't be tolerated even in Newgate, where only hardened felons were held.

"Here." She pushed a small purse through the bars. "It's all I have on me."

"My thanks."

"Thanks for nothing … call it a down-payment. If you succeed in the task we give you, we won't just pay your debt. There'll be a significant recompense. But trust me, captain, you'll have earned it. I must go now." Miss Evangeline moved away. "You'll hear from us very soon."

Sparrowhawk opened the purse; it contained four sovereigns, which was much more money than he'd seen in several months. His eyes bulged as he turned such riches over his hands. Then he glanced up and caught the turnkey eyeing them enviously. Clenching his fist, Sparrowhawk made to throw a punch through the bars. The turnkey went for his truncheon, but Sparrowhawk merely laughed, a sound that no-one in that place of lost and hopeless souls could remember when they'd last heard. The other prisoners watched in wonder as he made his way back to his cell, laughing all the way.

I

It was early in the morning, November 30th 1843, when John Sparrowhawk was taken from the Fleet Prison.

It was a bitterly cold day, the eaves of the surrounding tenements hung with icicles, the muddy gutters of Clerkenwell crackling with frost. The sky was pale grey, dots of snow spiralling down from it. The coachman was suitably attired: coated, gloved and muffled around his lower face. With his topper pulled down, only his nose was visible. He said nothing, but waited patiently. The door to his carriage, which was painted all over with black enamel, stood open on a plush interior.

Sparrowhawk, who'd emerged from the prison with a small sack of belongings and a blanket wrapped around him, climbed inside. The prison gate clanged shut, and the vehicle sped away. They drove straight to Westminster, halting at the rear of a tall, narrow building, which Sparrowhawk recognised as the hydropathic baths. Here, an attendant was waiting, a big, raw-boned fellow with thick, red whispers and braces over his linen undershirt. The tattoos on his brawny arms indicated a military background. When he spoke, it was with a Highlands accent.

"Captain Sparrowhawk, sir," he said. "My name's Angus. I'm to look after you today."

Sparrowhawk was led inside. He undressed in the changing room, and was given a loincloth and robe. He then watched bemusedly as Angus took his ragged prison garb out into the yard and poked it, piece by piece, into a lighted brazier.

"Filth, sir," Angus said by way of explanation. "No state of mind or manner of speech sets the poor man apart from the rich man as much as filth. We are like two nations in Britain today, those who are clean and those who are filthy. The sooner we break this barrier, the sooner we break the divide in our society."

Sparrowhawk was then sent into the first *caldarium*, a bare brick chamber with a tiled floor. He took off his robe and sat on a bench. The hot, dry air from the furnaces entered through vents near his feet, and swirled around him. It was the first time he'd been properly warm for nearly three months, but the painful tingle in his numbed extremities soon faded and he began to relax, imagining the dirt with which he'd been ingrained running away in trickles of sweat. After ten minutes, he went through to the second *caldarium*, where the temperature was much higher. Now he sweated feverishly, but it relaxed him even more. Prolonged extremes of heat are uncomfortable to many, but when you've been exposed to gnawing cold for so long – when you've slept under threadbare rags in a place where your vaporous breath hangs over you all night like a frozen shroud, when you've lived in a room where the damp on the inside walls regularly glistens with ice – you learn that you can never have too much of a good thing.

The atmosphere in the third *caldarium* exceeded 160 degrees. Even Sparrowhawk was only able to remain in there for a short time, but now his body was almost cleansed. The pores in his skin could breathe again. His hair, once filled with dust and spider-webs, was a wringing mop. He ran his fingers through it, rubbing his scalp with a scented salve that Angus had given him before entering, the burly Scot having promised that it would "do for all his ticks and lice".

After the *caldaria*, came the *frigidarium*, or cooling room, which contained the plunge pool. Here, he swam naked for a short time, before traipsing into the *hammam*, which was arched and decorated in the traditional eastern style. He lay face down on a wicker couch.

Most of the time in the Fleet Prison, there was naught to do but sleep. For many inmates this became pathological – it was simply too agonising to be awake. But in truth you never really slept. You were always half aware of your decayed surroundings, of the vermin scurrying over your prone body, of the vile wretches who might sneak upon you and pillage your paltry wares. You rarely, if ever, woke refreshed, before having to stumble through yet another torturous day in a state of semi-

11

torpor. Now at last, Sparrowhawk *did* sleep – or at least he was preparing to. When a pair of gentle hands began to manipulate his neck and shoulders, he all but sank into himself. Light, nimble fingers – he imagined they belonged to a woman, though of course such a thing would be most unseemly – worked expertly to loosen his knots of muscle.

"Miss Evangeline?" he breathed, delighted at the mere thought.

He pictured her leaning over him, clad only in petticoats and a bodice, the latter unlaced, the former clinging with sweat, her blonde ringlets hanging damp around her pretty face.

And then she dug her nails in, deeply.

He winced and grunted, but she dug all the harder, and suddenly there were claws affixed to his shoulders – not hands, but talons, which burrowed through the wasted flesh, rending and tearing at it viciously

Sparrowhawk knew the Turkish massage could be robust, but this was too much. One claw fastened onto the side of his neck, and started to squeeze. Again, sharp nails cut into him, clamping his throat, constricting his breath.

"Good God!" he gasped, twisting where he lay and looking around.

But no shampooer was present. Sparrowhawk lay alone.

He jumped up from the couch. The *hammam* was empty. One passage led off towards the smoking area, the other back to the *frigidarium*, the doorway to which was filled with opaque mist undisturbed by the passage of anyone. A bad dream, Sparrowhawk reflected. Surely no surprise after his ordeals of recent times? But when he touched his neck and shoulders, they were aching and bruised. He felt wheals in the skin. Angered, he went through into the *frigidarium*.

The plunge pool, the little he could see of it in the rolling vapour, was a glassy sheet; not a ripple broke its surface. There was no sound, save the dripping of condensation on the tiled floor. When he went back into the *hammam*, Angus had appeared, carrying a sponge thick with lather and a bundle of fluffy towels.

"Ready for your shampoo, sir?" the Scot asked.

"I thought I'd already had it," Sparrowhawk said.

"Not got round to you yet, sir. I have a couple of other customers to attend to as well."

"You have no other shampooers?"

"None on duty today, sir."

"You wouldn't by any chance employ a woman here?"

Angus looked shocked. "To work on a gentleman, sir? We'd have the police calling!"

"There are no women here at all?"

"Not today, sir. It's gentlemen only today."

Sparrowhawk said nothing more. He allowed himself to be 'shampooed', as the owners of these exotic establishments referred to it, this time properly, and if the Scot's vigorous attentions to his shoulders and neck caused him to flinch, he said nothing about it.

When his session was over, he was shown to a private room, where he was able to shave and don a suit of gentleman's clothes awaiting him on a hanger. In the inside pocket of the green frockcoat, he found a leather wallet containing thirty pounds. He was able to tip Angus from this, the overall fee apparently having been paid in advance by someone else.

Outside, it was snowing heavily and settling even the midst of London's swarming traffic. Across the road there was an inn, and in its downstairs window, lit by the ruddy flames of a log fire, Miss Evangeline was waiting at a private table.

"You look much better," she said when he entered. She indicted that he should sit. He noticed that knives, forks and napkins had been laid out for them both.

"These clothes are a little big on me," he said self-consciously.

"No matter. Your frame will soon fill out now that you've returned to normal life."

She'd dressed today in purple satin, her bonnet lavishly decorated with bows and ribbons; she looked quite dazzling.

Somewhat cowed by this, Sparrowhark removed his topper, and sat, regarding her warily. It suddenly seemed terribly unreal. Two days ago, he was a pauper who couldn't even afford his own freedom. Yet now he wore new leather shoes and white nankin trousers! His wallet clinked with silver!

"You've done so much for me," he said, "that I can't imagine what service you're expecting in return."

"I'll tell you duly," she replied. "But first let us eat."

Miss Evangeline was a remarkable woman in more ways than one. Despite her looks and youth – she was somewhere close to thirty, yet with the freshness and vitality of a schoolgirl – she was of a strong, independent spirit. Not only was she here in the middle of London without a chaperone (he assumed – a glance around the crowded interior revealed no-one showing interest in them), but she took it on herself to order their meal and, without consulting her male guest, asked also for a jug of mulled wine spiced with orange and cinnamon.

When the repast was set out, a haunch of venison, with a bowl of boiled potatoes and steamed carrots, Sparrowhawk gazed at it uncomprehendingly. For a man who recently had gnawed on black bread and drank melt-water from a cracked pipe, the aroma was almost overpowering. But how had such a change come about? He failed to understand, and when he didn't understand something it frightened him.

"Miss Evangeline," he said, "do you know who I actually am?"

"Of course." She carved him a portion of meat, ladled it with gravy and added vegetables. "Take some advice, if you would, captain. Though you may strongly be tempted, pray, don't wolf your food – your innards will be weakened by the rubbish you've been living on in the Fleet."

"Are you sure you know who I am?"

"I am fully aware of your history." She served herself a daintier portion.

"Miss Evangeline, I'm not just a war veteran and a debtor, I'm …"

"You're a widower," she interrupted, glancing up at him.

14

"Which is a surprise to no-one who knows you. You may not have murdered your wife, captain, but she died because you were an absolute swine to her." She watched him without blinking. "Is that what you wanted to hear?"

For some unfathomable reason, it didn't surprise him that she knew so much about him.

"I neglected her," he admitted.

"Oh, I think you did a little more than that." Miss Evangeline sat back in her chair, still watching him. "Such a sweet girl, Leticia, and so in love with you … to be repaid the way she was."

"I didn't, I never …" How often he'd used this defence, yet even when there was no-one to use it against save himself, it had never sounded genuine. "I never harmed her physically."

"No, but you didn't love her. And you rarely hesitated to show it."

He shrugged, indicating that he wasn't totally to blame. "I'd had no option but to marry her."

"You impregnated her, did you not? After the Grand Christmas Ball at Horse Guards."

"Marrying her was the honourable thing."

"Even though her family, the Frodshams, didn't want that for her? They disliked you so much as a military dissolute that they'd rather have lived with their daughter's shame."

"They didn't know me properly."

Miss Evangeline considered this. "Sometimes our reputations are not the whole story, I'll give you that. But what else were they to think, given that your own family had barely spoken to you in nearly two decades? Remind me what happened to the child."

"The child?"

"The reason you married Leticia."

"It … *he* died during birth."

"That must have been a blow to you both. Did you try for another?"

He wondered how she could ask such impertinent questions, much less how he could be answering them like this. And yet

15

there was nothing intense in her gaze – she hadn't mesmerised him, or hypnotised him. But she held him all the same with those lovely violet eyes.

"We didn't exactly try," he said.

"You weren't close physically?"

"Sometimes." He smiled with distant fondness, recalling his late wife's excitable manner and the delight in her face after the doctor's next visit. "Leticia never had a problem getting with child."

"No," Miss Evangeline said. "It was the delivering that was the problem, wasn't it? Your second child was a girl. I understand that she too died while trying to be born."

"Yes."

It surprised Sparrowhawk that he was suddenly blinking away tears. He hadn't thought there were any tears left in his body to cry.

"How did you respond to that, captain?"

"I left."

"Left?"

"I went abroad with my regiment."

"Hmm." Miss Evangeline pondered. "An odd thing for a husband to do with his wife in such a pitiful state."

"There was war. I was being deployed to Afghanistan."

"Ahhh now … Captain Sparrowhawk, our relationship will not blossom if you lie to me. You weren't being deployed to Afghanistan, were you? You volunteered."

"I had skills that were needed."

"Nevertheless, you *volunteered*. No-one would have thought the less of you if you hadn't gone."

"I had no idea how badly Leticia was hurt."

"What did you expect?"

"She only took ill after I'd left."

"Almost straight away after. When it suddenly dawned on her that she would not be seeing you again for a very considerable time."

He regarded the victuals on his plate. The meat was cooling,

16

the gravy congealing. For months he'd been gaunt with hunger, watering at the gills just imagining food – but now he had no appetite for anything.

"If you know all this about me," he said, "why on Earth are you employing me?"

"Why indeed? Well ... as I said before, Captain Sparrowhawk, you may be a very inadequate man. But on the other hand you were a very good soldier. And it's the soldier we're interested in at present."

She raised her goblet in toast to him. But she wasn't smiling. And only now did he fully understand that, whatever she had in mind for him, it would be no jolly holiday.

II

That night, Sparrowhawk suffered another strange occurrence, this one of an even less benign sort – as Miss Evangeline had forecast that he probably would.

"You must protect someone," she said during the afternoon, as they drove towards an address in Camden Town that had been rented for him.

"Who?" he asked.

"Nobody of significance. Just an ordinary man."

"I don't understand."

"He lives in a house in Bloomsbury. You don't need to know his name. All you need to know is that he'll need protection during the first three weeks of December."

"Only the first three weeks?"

"Yes. From that point on, others will take charge."

Sparrowhawk pondered this. "Who wishes him ill?"

"Again, I can't give you a name. But three individuals will attempt to attack him at his home during the hours of darkness."

"I still don't understand."

"Three visitants – each of a distinctly unpleasant nature – will come. They will come separately, and each will make one attempt to enter the premises. You must stop them all."

"Miss Evangeline, I need to know more if I'm to do a proper job."

"I can't tell you any more at present, but take this." She handed him an envelope. "There are several addresses in here. Inns and eating houses where you might contact me during the course of the mission. There is also a residential address where you might find me quickly should the need arise, though I can't stress enough that this must only occur if it is absolutely necessary. There is also the address of the man you must protect. Keep vigil at his house every night, from tomorrow onwards until December 21st, and if he is unharmed by that date your task will be complete."

Sparrowhawk opened the envelope. Inside, as she had said, there was a printed card bearing various addresses. The two that interested him most were Miss Evangeline's 'residential address', which was *13, Rislington Row, Eastcheap,* a surprisingly seedy district, in his opinion, and the address he was to defend: *48, Doughty Street, Bloomsbury.*

"It would help immeasurably if I knew the opposition," he said.

"I can only tell you that they will strike hard and in, shall we say, *unusual* ways. It's also possible that you won't see them until they are right upon you, so you must be watchful all the time."

He gazed at her. "This is ridiculous. An enemy whose strength and disposition are unknown to me? An enemy I can't even see…?"

"How often did you see the Ghilazi tribesmen until they were ready? When you set out from Kabul to Jellalabad with more women and children in your column than fellow soldiers, had you any idea you'd be facing a foe fifty thousand strong?"

He hesitated to reply as unpleasant memories were stirred. Outside, it was already growing dark. Snow fell heavily and steadily, London's working population thronging through it as they made their way home, wrapped in plumes of smoky breath. Fleetingly they were wraiths: ragged stick figures trudging through a dark and desolate land. It was the retreat from Kabul all over again, the British army and their dependents straggling for miles along icy, muddy tracks, frozen and starved, incessantly harried by packs of Afghan horsemen, their corpses littering the wayside.

"If all I have to do is stand guard at night, I can manage that," he finally said.

"There is one other thing, captain – this man must not know you are there."

"Come again?"

"He must never be aware of you."

"But that makes no sense."

"Watch the house. Do not under any circumstance announce

yourself. If you do that for any reason – any reason at all – I will bill your bail straight back to the debtors' court and you will be re-arrested and forced to serve the remainder of your sentence."

Sparrowhawk was baffled. "Won't it help him to know? Give him some reassurance that he's safe?"

"He needs no reassurance because he doesn't know that he is in danger. If you inform him, however, things may alter dramatically and for the worse."

Sparrowhawk peered out into the winter gloom.

At length, he said: "No."

She glanced round at him. "Excuse me?"

"I won't do it." He shook his head, quite firmly. "You're asking too much. Taking me from the frying pan into the fire and expecting me thank you for it. Miss Evangeline … I'm a soldier, not a night watchman. To give an adequate level of protection, I need intelligence on my enemy. I don't consider that an unreasonable request, and, if you and your masters do, I think I'm better off in the Fleet than serving whatever futile cause you've been trusted with."

She regarded him carefully, and sighed.

"The most I can tell you is that this man is engaged in a project on our behalf – very secret and very important. This is why you must guard him. The party I represent would have a very difficult time if this project were interrupted."

"You said I'd be recompensed. How much?"

"Your lodgings are paid for in advance – at least until Christmastide is over. Plus you'll have living expenses throughout December. A final fee will be paid to you on completion of the work, but that will of course depend on your performance."

"No man ever agreed to such a thing."

"No man ever was released from the debtor's prison without having paid a penny of the debt himself."

Their carriage trundled beneath a brick arch and arrived in a courtyard surrounded by tall, narrow buildings. Some of the lower windows were broken and boarded. Only a few of those upstairs had lights in them. Sparrowhawk made to climb out, but Miss Evangeline put a hand on his arm.

"Stay alert, captain. Even during daylight when you're off duty. Once you've been identified as a threat, you too may receive unwanted visits."

"Your concern charms me." He jumped down into the snow. "I'll keep an eye open."

"Keep both open. This enemy is very clever."

"They'll need to be cleverer than this morning."

"This morning?" She sounded puzzled.

"Some wretch tried to strangle me in the bathhouse. But all they managed to hurt was my pride because I was caught napping."

"Then it's begun already." She looked troubled, even alarmed.

"Don't worry about me," he said. "Just tell these people – I understand espionage and I refuse to believe you haven't got a channel of communication to them – that the next one who comes had better be armour-plated. I won't be caught twice."

But later that night it wasn't quite so simple.

Sparrowhawk's quarters were a suite of three drab rooms, which he found at the top of a damp, rickety stair. They were clean enough, but only minimally furnished, with frayed rugs over their bare floorboards. However there were two fireplaces, both stacked with coal and kindling, and in the bedroom a narrow but comfortable bed, which looked and smelled as if it had been made up with fresh bedding. Alongside it was a dresser, and on this a bowl of water – and if the water had frozen over, which it had, Sparrowhawk didn't suppose he could really lay the blame for that at the door of his benefactors. There was also a wardrobe, containing several changes of clothing. None of these were expensive; in fact all erred towards the rougher, readier end of the market – which made sense. It would be less easy for a dandy to blend into the city's dark places. The third room was a small scullery. It wasn't exactly crammed to bursting, but there were pots and pans in there, cutlery and various tinned consumables on its shelves, plus a stack of candles. Some thoughtful soul had also left him a pipe, a wedge of tobacco and a small bottle of French brandy. As promised, there was enough money for him to get by over the next few days.

He lit a fire in the living room, boiled himself some porridge, pulled the easy chair in front of the flames and set a match to his pipe. His preferred means of smoking was the cigar – in particular the Cuban cheroot – but his funds didn't run to such luxuries at present. Gradually the room warmed up, and he found himself sliding into a snooze.

The December wind wailed in the chimney, causing the flames to flare in the grate. Beyond the curtained casements, he imagined billions of snowflakes tumbling over the jumbled roofs and chimneys of London. By now, it would be unbearably cold in the bowels of the Fleet. Many of its inmates wouldn't survive these bitter months; each morning they'd be brought out blue in the face, rigid as boards, and tossed like trash into a pauper's grave. Harsh, unrelenting cold was something he'd become accustomed to during his many sojourns along the Khyber Pass, but there was no guarantee that he himself could have avoided such a fate if he'd stayed in prison. His good fortune to be taken from that place of desolation could not be overstated, but then he recalled Miss Evangeline's concern when he'd told her about the incident in the bathhouse, and he wondered about the nameless foe that alarmed her so much.

And that was when he heard the first creak on the stair. It was nothing, he surmised – a shutter tapping in the blizzard, woodwork contracting with the cold. But then a second creak followed, and a third. They were footfalls.

Sparrowhawk leapt to his feet.

The door to his apartment was closed and locked, but so was the door downstairs, the outer door connecting with the courtyard. Nobody could have entered unless they had a key. He briefly relaxed. Miss Evangeline probably – she'd told him that she was the only other key-holder to this property. But now more footfalls ascended. And these weren't the dainty tread of a lady – they were heavy, uncoordinated *clumps*, made by more than one pair of feet.

He grabbed the fire-poker, and stood ready.

That these people, whoever they were, had caught up with him in the Turkish bath didn't say much for Miss Evangeline's level of security. But their closing in on his private lodgings, and so quickly, suggested that it was virtually nonexistent. He would have to take that up with her. He moved to the door. Putting his ear to the wood, he now heard only silence on the other side – almost as if whoever was out there was aware that he was listening and had paused – only for them to proceed up again, clumping, stumbling loudly, maybe seven or eight pairs of feet all at the same time. Sparrowhawk pictured boots, caked not just with ice and snow but with mud and blood, maybe bound with filthy, gangrenous rags.

Raising the poker to his shoulder, he backed into the room, pushing the chair out of his way to give himself space. It occurred to him that if they were armed – maybe with the new Brunswick rifles – they could shoot clean through the door, so he stepped to one side. But again the feet, now apparently at the top of the stair, halted. A prolonged silence followed.

Despite the warmth of the fire, Sparrowhawk felt an eerie chill. He hardly dared breathe as he strained his ears for any muffled conversation. Why were they waiting? Were there more of them yet to come up? He realised that he would have to take the initiative. Whoever they were, they were bottled up on the narrow stair. That way he could meet them one at a time instead of all at once. And they had another disadvantage: the first to be flung back down would take several of the others with him. Sparrowhawk advanced to the door, wiping his moist palms on his waistcoat. He paused one more time to listen – still there was silence on the other side. He couldn't imagine who they might be. They could be half-dead with cold for all he knew. Their clumsy ascent had indicated men in some way exhausted or disoriented.

As bewildered as he was frightened, he turned the lock and yanked the door open.

The landing beyond was empty.

He stepped forwards and peered down the stair. It was pitch black down there, but pale light – reflecting from the gas lamp in the snowy courtyard – poked in pencil-thin shafts around the outer door. No skulking or crouching figures blocked it.

Sparrowhawk's hair prickled. He knew that he hadn't imagined those stomping feet. His years of front line service had allowed him to distinguish in an instant the difference between dream and reality. He rushed to his mantel, took a candle, lit it and went back to the stair. The flame cast luminescence all the way to the bottom. There was definitely nobody there, though he sniffed at the air and fancied there was a vague, unpleasant smell reminiscent of rotting flesh.

He descended to the bottom. The outer door rattled as the wind battered it. But this too was locked, and not just by his key. Both the upper and lower bolts were rammed home – exactly as he'd left them earlier. No-one could have entered, and certainly they could not have entered and left again.

Sparrowhawk returned to his rooms, closing and locking the door behind him. He wondered briefly about the assailant in the bathhouse and how strange it was that he too had vanished without trace. And then he spotted the large bold message, which, in his brief absence downstairs, had been inscribed on the wall above his fireplace. He approached it slowly, eyes goggling – before going around the rest of his rooms like a whirlwind, searching every nook and cranny but finding nothing. He checked all his windows, but they too were locked. Outside, the streets were deserted. Scarcely a track – either of man, animal or cartwheel – was visible in the crisp new blanket of snow. On legs so shaky they could barely support him, he moved back to the fireplace. The message had been made by a finger dipped in ordure or blood, or a foul mixture of both. It read:

SEASON'S GREETINGS

III

The following day, December 1ˢᵗ, was pitilessly cold, though crisp and clear.

Sparrowhawk, who had barely slept owing to the events of the previous night, rose at about six and set off on foot for Whitechapel. He was attired in 'working' garb of scuffed boots, worn trousers, a woollen undershirt, a waistcoat and a neckerchief. Over the top of that, he'd donned gloves, a weather-beaten greatcoat with a double cape at its shoulders, and a crumpled topper.

Though it was a bitter day, London life passed him by as normal, the wagons and carts churning up fountains of muddy snow, straw and dung. As well as working folk, there were beggars aplenty, the blind and the lame rattling their tin cups for alms, and then the costermongers – the hawkers and street sellers – haranguing the public from their barrows, selling everything from eel soup to pigs' trotters, from lemonade to kitchen grease, from frogs, lizards and snails to 'rare and exotic birds', most of which would be sparrows and finches done up with colourful paint. At the corner of Petticoat Lane, the Old Clothes Exchange, or the 'Rag Fair' as it was known, backed up against the East India Company warehouses. Old garments were heaped higgledy-piggledy along the pavements here. Coats and shabby jackets hung in every doorway or from wooden stalls, which the more prosperous vendors had been able to set up. There were piles of boots, shoes and hats, tattered brollies, broken walking sticks. Crowds of prospective buyers milled about, haggling with the sellers. Despite the chill, a stench of sweat and unwashed bodies arose from the bundles of second-hand clothing.

Using this organised chaos as cover, Sparrowhawk sidled into a pawn brokerage, turning its 'open' sign to 'closed' before shutting its barred door behind him. It was a dingy, cluttered place divided in two by a high counter. The small space afforded for those seeking loans was unheated, its concrete floor puddled where the snow had melted from countless pairs of leaky shoes. Behind the counter, the pawnbroker was perched on a high stool. He was a broad, pudgy man with a red complexion, bloated cheeks and a long, woodpecker nose on the end of which a pair of *prince nez* were balanced. He had a colossal thatch of ginger hair, hanks of which hung from either side of his face, and fat hands covered with cheap rings. He wore a large, shapeless garment, rather like a housecoat but covered with eastern designs, and an emerald-green cravat. When Sparrowhawk entered, the pawnbroker was scratching in a ledger with a quill. To one side of him, a stove roared noisily, ensuring that he at least had warmth.

Sparrowhawk produced a grubby ticket, and placed it on the counter. The pawnbroker said nothing, but continued to write. He didn't even glance up. His attention was only caught when Sparrowhawk produced a small purse filled with coins, and placed that alongside the ticket.

After a brief, studied silence, the broker withdrew into a darkened recess, where he rummaged around for several minutes. When he returned, he had a locked iron strongbox, which he opened with a key attached to a jangling key ring at his belt. From out of the box, he took three items. The first was a leather bolster, the sort of thing normally attached to a saddle. It was fastened with two buckles, but it bulged almost to capacity, as well it might containing eighty brass cartridges of heavy-grain buckshot. The second was a cavalry sabre, which had been broken half way down the blade, but expertly re-honed to sharpness, so that it was now more like a large, guard-hilted knife. The third was a double-barrelled Greener shotgun, a shortened twelve-bore breechloader, made from walnut wood and horn steel, its lockwork beautifully engraved with images of game.

Before handing these over, the broker checked in his ledger and said in a thin voice: "You had another ticket, of course. If you've lost it, no matter. The item still resides in my store room – a velvet pouch containing several campaign medals and ribbons."

"I didn't lose the ticket," Sparrowhawk said. "I threw it away.

Keep the medals. Sell them. They'll fetch you a decent price."

The broker eyed him curiously, and then shrugged. "As you wish." He emptied the purse and counted its contents. But when he'd finished, he sniffed disapprovingly. "Not enough, I'm afraid."

Sparrowhawk was shocked. "What's that?"

"There is twenty-five pounds here. Including interest, the full redemption price for these weapons is thirty."

"That's quite a mark-up," Sparrowhawk said. "And it's not what we agreed."

"Nevertheless, those are my terms. Someone else will take them, I'm sure."

"You thieving, conniving …"

"Spare me your moral outrage, Sparrowhawk. You think I routinely hold items like these as collateral? There was no little risk involved, and I don't like risks."

"Thirty pounds." Sparrowhawk scowled, filching an extra five-pound note from his breeches pocket and handing it over.

The pawnbroker smiled and pushed the goods across his desk. "Isn't it a price worth paying for extra security?"

Sparrowhawk slid the Greener and the sabre under his greatcoat, and thought again about the incident the previous night. "Maybe."

"Think yourself lucky I took them at all. I don't normally deal with criminals."

"Neither did I until today."

From Whitechapel, he headed south to the river, entering that district of dockland known as the 'Pool of London', which lay between Execution Dock in the east and Billingsgate Market in the west. Again despite the cold, it was a bustling scene, the churning waterway alive with traffic of every description, from tugs and paddle-steamers, to passenger ferries, coal barges and full-sized cargo vessels. Both shorelines, north and south, were forests of masts and rigging, the quays laden with all manner of goods, from mountains of sea-produce, to crates, barrels, chests, sacks of corn and great glittering mounds of coal. Folk of every sort were employed here: tars and riggers, lightermen, watermen, ballast-heavers, porters and warehousemen, the usual glut of hucksters and hawkers mingling among them, selling everything from oysters and whelks, to beer and fresh 'backy'. The noise was fit to deafen a man: horns, sirens and bells, the crash and bang of the lumper gangs, the creak and grind of cranes and pulleys, and the wild, enthusiastic shouting of the river-traders: "Purl ahoy, purl ahoy!"; "Skate 'n' haddock, ha'penny each!"; "Nice glass o' peppermint for ya, wash the salt away!"

Sparrowhawk wound patiently through this bedlam, at last crossing the river by London Bridge, and entering Southwark, where, in the looming shadow of the Marshalsea Prison, another high walled hellhole for the retirement of debtors, lay the animal pens, the slaughter yards, and the ultimate object of his journey, the horse fair. After wandering the paddocks for half an hour, and browsing the available beasts, he selected a piebald mare, about four years old, whose name was 'Peppercorn'. He paid for the hire of the animal for one month, with a view to extending this and maybe purchasing her if she gave him satisfaction.

"She likes you, sir," laughed the toothless young Irish merchant, as the animal nudged Sparrowhawk in the back while he signed the papers. "She don't do that for everyone."

Sparrohawk patted the animal, and groomed her between the ears to calm her.

"You know your way round horses," the Irishman observed.

"I ought to."

"You don't own one yourself, sir?"

"Not since I had to put the last one down."

"Ahhh! Tis always a sad time, is that."

"On this occasion it was a relief." Sparrowhawk tried not to flinch at the memory. "She'd just had three of her legs blown off."

IV

Sparrowhawk slept for most of the afternoon. Partly this was to catch up on sleep lost the previous night, but also it was a conscious decision to adjust his 'body clock'.

After he'd woken and eaten, he stashed his weapons beneath his coat in a harness that he'd fashioned from linen strips, collected Peppercorn from a stable yard three streets away, where he'd a rented a stall, and headed out of Camden Town.

Dusk descended and snow was falling again, as he entered the more moneyed district of Bloomsbury. Doughty Street was a row of tall, three-story townhouses facing onto a small park. Decorative wreathes were already displayed on several of its front doors. At one gas-lit corner, a horde of well-wrapped children danced and pirouetted around a grizzled old fellow with a barrel organ, cranking out a less than harmonious version of *In Dulci Jubilo*. For a brief moment, the sight of the prancing youngsters reminded Sparrowhawk of his own two children, neither of whom had lived to see even one Christmas. Likewise, the house, number 48, was similar to the house he'd owned in Little Chelsea, and shared for several years with Leticia. Darkness was gathering, however, and he managed to shake these thoughts from his mind. He tethered Peppercorn under the park's bandstand shelter, and commenced a foot patrol of the district. Number 48 had only one other approach apart from the front, and that was at the back, where its small rear garden ended in a high wall. Behind that, there was a narrow access passage. Sparrowhawk would have to move constantly between the two, to ensure that both these approaches were covered, but to be on the safe side he removed a number of dustbin lids and propped them up against the footing of the garden wall; that way, if someone tried to scramble over it in the darkness, at least one or two lids would be knocked over and create a *clatter*.

At length, satisfied that he'd looked the neighbourhood over thoroughly, he installed himself in the park, to wait. Snow came down in a steady cascade, muffling all sounds of the city. Gradually, those few hardy souls left outside retreated indoors. Soon there was a deadening hush, the only sound the steady *hiss* of settling flakes.

Sparrowhawk gazed at the front of the house through a mass of rhododendrons. Its curtained windows emanated a warm, rosy light. With the wreathe on the door, it was like a scene from a Christmas card. Aside from a parlour maid, who appeared briefly to beat a doormat, he hadn't seen any of the occupants, though he had no doubt that some of those were children – there were occasional bursts of shrill laughter from the upper stories. He thought again of Little Chelsea, and in particular the winter's day when he'd returned there from the Afghan campaign, not so much triumphant as bone-weary, exhausted, sickened by killing. Still on crutches, stiff, weakened by slow-healing wounds and the fever he'd incurred on the appallingly cramped troopship, he'd climbed from his carriage to find a house empty and silent. No servants rushed out to help with his baggage. There was no cheering, no loving kiss on the battle-scarred cheek. Instead of Union Jacks, his house was bedecked with black curtains of mourning.

"Someone should have informed me beforehand that Leticia was dead," he said half-aloud. "I was her husband. I had a right to know."

So many months later, the feeling of loss surprised him. Yes, he'd been selfish, arrogant, callous beyond belief with his young wife. But she'd been a sweet child, so content to be with him, so eager to please, so desperate for his love and adoration. How could one not feel affection under those circumstances? And now she was gone – a memory, nothing more. His wretched in-laws had even refused to tell him where they'd buried her.

He was distracted from these thoughts by a noise from the rear of the property – a distinct *clang* of metal. Instantly, he came alert. Creeping across the park to the gas-lamp, he checked his pocket watch. It wasn't yet nine o'clock. It seemed too early for any kind of criminal activity. Nearly all the houses were still illuminated, but he had to investigate. He moved across Doughty Street and circled to the rear of the terraced row. As he did, a sleek tomcat needled past him, stopping to purr and wrap its silky form around his legs. When he checked in the alley, one of the dustbin lids had shifted, but a neat set of paw prints snaked past it in the snow.

Unwilling simply to plant himself in the park and wait all night, Sparrowhawk recommenced another patrol, surveying every conceivable road and avenue connecting with Doughty Street, so that not a single hiding place was invisible to him. A couple of time he went to a grating where warm vapours were rising, but only occasionally. As he'd found in Afghanistan, his body needed to harden to the rigours of the cold, his senses to acclimatise. To constantly seek solace in warmth would leave him sluggish and despondent whenever he had to return to the chill.

By late evening, the streets had been empty for several hours, though on one occasion Sparrowhawk had to hide when a strolling constable came by. Dressed as he was, his loitering in a district like this would certainly arouse suspicion. At around midnight the snow stopped falling. The clouds cleared, to leave a sky of black silk spangled with winter stars. By now, the lights in the row of houses had all been extinguished. London was asleep.

Sparrohawk might have nodded off too, but occasionally he had the feeling he was being watched. This was another extra-sensory skill he'd perfected during his years in the Colours. He'd never worked out whether there was a scientific basis to it, or merely his overwrought imagination, but it never paid to ignore such warnings. Several times he was convinced that someone was directly behind him. He would always whirl around, his right hand going for the hilt of his Greener. But each time the park looked desolate and empty beneath its mantel of snow, its bushes limned black and skeletal on the moonlit whiteness. The only movement back there was from Peppercorn, standing under the bandstand cover, snuffling in a fog of her own breath – until

31

about one o'clock in the morning, when something else caught Sparrowhawk's eye. At first he only glimpsed it, and then he thought he was seeing things. But when he looked again, there was no question. Two blots of darkness had detached themselves from a shadowed doorway at the far end of Doughty Street, and were now prowling slowly up it.

Sparrowhawk crouched.

Closer up, the two figures wore heavy coats, which almost covered their entire bodies, and woollen hoods pulled over their heads. It gave them an unearthly appearance. They were like phantoms; if it hadn't been for their crunching footfalls, he'd have sworn they were gliding over the snow rather than walking. They moved side by side, their shoulders hunched, and didn't speak until they reached a point directly opposite number 48, where they paused and mumbled together. One of them then remained where he was, glancing from side to side, while the other crossed the road and rounded the corner of the terrace. A few moments later, the other reappeared and signalled his mate, who scampered across the road to join him. They both vanished from view again, but not before the second man's left hand slipped into view, holding what looked like a pistol.

Sparrowhawk quickly forged his way through the bushes, clambered over the railing, and followed them across the road. When he reached the corner of the terrace, he heard the dull impact of a boot on a snowy dustbin lid. He sidled to the alley entrance and glanced down it. The hooded shapes were braced against the rear wall of number 48. One had made a stirrup with his hands for the other to climb up and over.

Sparrowhawk knew he had to make an immediate decision. He was under strict instructions that the occupants of the house were not to be alerted. That meant he must fight these transgressors somewhere else, which would be a good idea for other reasons, too. Miss Evangeline had said there would be three visitants, so, even if that was their total number and they had no auxiliaries at all, they weren't all present – he needed to know who and where the other was, and, if possible, exactly how many members there were in this gang. Close beside him there was a row of privets with bars in front of them. He ran the blade of his sabre along them, the way he'd seen constables do with their truncheons. He also began to whistle loudly – *In Dulci Jubilo* again, just like a lonely peeler roaming his midnight beat. He did this for precisely fifteen seconds, before moving back to the mouth of the alley. As he'd expected, the figures of the two men were already at the far end, running for their lives.

He dashed back across the park to the bandstand, mounting Peppercorn and urging her to a canter. Even in glistening starlight, it was too dark in the alley to see the two men's tracks in the snow, but when they emerged at the far end onto the wider thoroughfares, it became easy: firstly because almost nobody else had been out and about since the last snowfall; secondly because, if all else failed, Sparrowhawk had been one of the most celebrated trackers in the 16th Light Dragoons.

He followed them at his own pace for several miles, heading through Clerkenwell and St Luke's, and eventually into Hoxton, where the ways became narrow and twisting, passing between rookeries that reeked of squalour and villainy. There was no atmosphere of the approaching season in this neighbourhood. The poor had little time for such frivolousness as Christmas. They had next to no money to spend on it. They were granted almost no holiday with which to enjoy it. The birth of the Saviour seemed to have made no difference at all to the miseries of their world. Increasingly, most of them felt that Christmas didn't extend to them at all – why should they even respect it, let alone celebrate it?

Despite having no heat and probably no light in the hovels they called their homes, the chill had kept most of this distract indoors, so the trail remained clear and Sparrowhawk was able to follow it easily – though at one point there was a disturbance where some violent incident had occurred. Slumped against a wall nearby was an elderly fellow. Most likely, he'd been wending his drunken way home when he'd met with the two rogues. Sparrowhawk dismounted, and looked him over. He was still alive, but bleeding copiously from the nose and mouth. His pockets had been torn inside out, and presumably divested of anything valuable. The loose end of a watch chain was visible, the watch having been snapped free.

"You all right, sir?" Sparrowhawk asked, tapping the old man's cheek to try and wake him.

The man stirred and grunted. When he opened his mouth, his alcohol-laced breath was sickening. Sparrowhawk helped him to his feet and pushed him on his way, saying: "Mind you get home quickly now. Wash those cuts."

The man said something incoherent, but lumbered off into the darkness. Sparrowhawk re-mounted and continued to follow the tracks – for another few hundred yards, again diverting along crooked defiles cluttered with bones and snow-covered rubbish. He finally arrived on some open waste ground, in the centre of which sat a small, ramshackle building: a timber, one-storey affair, little more than a hut with a sagging tarpaper roof. Its windows were thick with grime, and in most cases broken. Dirty sheets had been hung over the inside of them, but firelight still shone through. Overhead, a rusted metal chimney pumped brackish smoke.

Sparrowhawk tethered Peppercorn in the adjoining passage, before making a reconnaissance on foot. He saw that there was only one door to the building, which served his purpose. In addition, the open space all around was conveniently cluttered with barrels, empty crates and the like, providing plenty of opportunities for cover.

It was only possible to see through one of the windows, where a sheet had not been hung properly. From the glimpse he had, it was a typical thieves' kitchen. A total of six men were in there, but whether young or old it was difficult to say. All were dirty and ragged, with matted mops of hair and the feral expressions of dogs. One sat cross-legged by a coal fire, scraping food from a plate. Another stooped over a table, picking through an open strongbox; from the occasional glint, its contents comprised coins and jewellery. The others were lounging on stools, smoking pipes or sipping from mugs. One had removed his heavy coat, but beneath it was wearing a woollen seaman's jerkin, the hood of which Sparrowhawk clearly recognised. He smiled to himself, only to then spot something that stiffened his spine.

A seventh person was in the room, a young girl clad only in underwear, which was torn and dirty, and bloodied around the crotch. She was bruised and thin, and had been forced to sit with her back to a wooden beam, which her arms had been bound around with tight cords. A handkerchief had been fixed over her eyes as a blindfold.

Now knowing he had an even more urgent task, Sparrowhawk backed from the window and scanned the surrounding area, making sure that he knew his battleground. He found a heavy piece of slate and, manoeuvring a barrel against the side of the hut, used it to clamber onto the roof. He belly-crawled to the apex, and placed the slate across the top of the chimney. Sliding back down, he retreated to a distance of about twelve yards from the door. He broke his Greener to ensure it was loaded, snapped it closed again, and dropped to a crouch behind an empty crate.

It took longer than he'd expected before there was a commotion inside. The door to the hut finally burst open, and two of the men came staggering out in a cloud of smoke.

Sparrowhawk fired twice: two booming detonations in the frosty air.

Both payloads struck clean. The first man was slammed sideways against the wall; the second was smashed back in through the open door.

"Season's greetings!" Sparrowhawk bellowed, rolling from his position and reloading.

Smoke still gouted from the open doorway. There was frenzied coughing and now a wild shouting. Two more figures appeared there, gagging, half-blinded, but hesitant to come out.

35

One of these was the man who'd had the pistol on Doughty Street. He took a shot at the crate where Sparrowhawk had formerly been kneeling. Sparrowhawk, now yards away from there, fired both barrels again, this time from a prone position.

A doorjamb tore free in a blizzard of splintered woodwork. Both men were struck, one catapulting out into the open, landing face first in the snow, his head and upper body shredded by shot. The second, the pistol man, caromed sideways and fell, clutching at a wound in his side from which steamy breath was visibly venting.

Sparrowhawk jumped up and dashed forwards, breaking the shotgun again and reloading it, and barging his way into the hut.

It stank in there: sweat, grime, urine, stale alcohol. But clouds of smoky fumes were billowing from the fireplace, almost filling the room. As he'd expected, the remaining two thieves had been preparing their hostage as a human shield. They'd loosened her from the beam and lifted her to her feet, but her terror had given her courage. She wrestled with them, and shrieked as she coughed. They shrieked back, and also coughed, their eyes streaming. One of them – a tall, cadaverous horror with brown 'fang' teeth, sunken eyes and a pockmarked face – spotted Sparrowhawk. He immediately lunged to the table, grabbed a blunderbuss and, snatching a handful of nails, crammed them into its barrel. But before he could aim, the Greener's stock had slammed into his face, shattering his teeth and almost toppling him over. He tried to turn and stagger away, but Sparrowhawk levelled the Greener and fired, blowing him clean in half, spraying the fireplace with gore and guts.

The last of the thieves was younger, with flaxen rat-tails for hair and horrific facial scars. He shoved the girl aside and flung a heavy stool, which knocked the Greener to the floor. Howling, he ripped a cutlass from his belt, and charged. Drawing his own blade, Sparrowhawk parried the first blow, swerved around his assailant, and rammed the sabre into his back, wrenching it upwards and sideways, so that a mass of vital organs flopped out.

Ashen-faced, the thief dropped his cutlass, but still tried to grapple with Sparrowhawk, clutching at his lapels as he sank to his knees. Sparrowhawk yanked the thief's head back by the hair, and cut his throat.

Throughout all this, the girl, too terrorised to remove her blindfold, stood stock still, alternately wailing and choking. Sparrowhawk spun around to ensure that he hadn't missed anyone, grabbed up his Greener, threw a blanket over the girl's shoulders and propelled her outside.

The pistol man was still alive, albeit lying on his back in agony. Despite his pitted face and blood-clotted whiskers, this thief was almost handsome; he was about thirty, and looked physically strong. Most likely he was a leader here, and for that reason Sparrowhawk knelt and cut his throat as well, before ushering the girl away.

"Who are you?" he asked her, as they entered the passage where Peppercorn was waiting.

"Mi … mi … mi name's Judd, sir," she stammered, either the cold or fear, or both, making it difficult to understand her. "Am … Amy Judd …"

By her accent, she was a native of inner London, though not a child of its streets.

"And what are you?"

"Sc … scullery maid, sir."

"How did those scoundrels get hold of you?"

"Mi … mi father's a gambling man, sir. He owes money. He wouldn't pay, so Klebworth took me instead." She began to cry. "And they took me too, sir. Him an' his gang. So many times …"

"Well the ordeal's over now, girl. You're safe …"

"Sir, c … can I please take this blindfold off?"

"No!" He shouted, more forcefully than he'd intended. It set her crying all the harder. "Ease off the noise, girl. We need to get away from here. Just stay as you are for the time being. Where does your father live?"

"Just … just off the Ratcliffe Highway, sir."

Sparrowhawk cursed. The Ratcliffe Highway was a considerable distance away.

"I'm … I'm sure I can walk there on my own, sir …"

"I'll take you, but leave your blindfold on."

He tried to help her onto the horse, but it was awkward. She'd been grievously injured between her legs and couldn't straddle the beast, so she had to ride side-saddle, perched on his lap. This was not ideal, for the gunfire had now drawn attention from the surrounding buildings, and they'd have to ride swiftly. However, he kept a firm grip on her as they galloped south, and even managed to draw the blanket more closely around her shivering form.

"Lord … lord bless you, sir," she whimpered. "Are you a constable?"

"I'm nobody," he replied.

"Don't say that, sir …"

"I'm nobody, you understand? Nobody came to help you, nobody has rescued you, nobody is taking you home!"

She nodded, but fresh tears seeped through the handkerchief, and it was a relief for him when they reached the Ratcliffe Highway. He reined Peppercorn alongside a gin shop, in the upper apartment of which lights were already burning – the docklands were always the first part of London to come to life. Hurriedly, he let her down.

"Count to twenty before you remove that blindfold," he instructed.

She nodded dumbly.

"And before I leave, mind you warn your father that he doesn't place another bet until he's used some of his pay to get a doctor to see you … you understand? Or else Nobody will return to the Ratcliffe Highway very promptly."

He wheeled the horse around and cantered hard to the west, snow flying behind him. He glanced back once before veering into a side-alley. The girl was under a gaslight, tentatively removing her blindfold.

Urging the animal on, he vanished into the shadows.

V

The following noon, Sparrowhawk attended one of the luncheon houses specified on Miss Evangeline's list. It was a smart establishment located on High Holborn.

He ordered pork chops, devilled kidneys and a small bottle of wine. He was mid-way through this repast when Miss Evangeline arrived at the entrance to his booth, unannounced but looking delightful in a fur cap, kid gloves and green taffeta cloak over a flower printed muslin dress. She again smelled sweetly of rose and jasmine. However, her attitude was cool. She did not return his smile, but laid that day's *Illustrated London News* on his table. Its front-page story told of:

Ghastly incident: half a dozen slain

Mr. Cruikshank had provided a sketch detailing a squalid hovel with broken windows, outside of which three corpses lay covered with cloth, and three po-faced police gentlemen stood scratching their prominent chins, while behind them a variety of demonic, jack-o-lantern faces peeked around corners. The caption read:

The impossible happens: Hoxton gets more horrible

"This wasn't what we hired you to do," she said.

Sparrowhawk offered her some wine, but she declined.

"I've always been proactive, Miss Evangeline. As soon as I got the scent, I carried the battle to them. Attack is the best form of defence. Surely you've heard that said?"

"I have indeed."

"Then why so glum? Your man is now safe, two and a half weeks earlier than expected."

"Except that he isn't safe," she said, sitting facing him. "Because James Klebworth's gang had nothing to do with the task we set you."

40

Momentarily, Sparrowhawk was lost for words. "But they were armed. They attempted to break into 48, Doughty Street."

"They were common burglars. Nothing more."

"Let me get this straight, I killed the wrong people last night?"

"Yes. Six of them to be precise."

He pondered this, but then shook his head, dismissing any fleeting concern. "There was a hostage in there, a haul of goods and gold. They must have been cracking houses for years."

"That's irrelevant. The law would have dealt with them in due course."

"Where 48, Doughty Street is concerned, Miss Evangeline, I deem myself the law." He continued to eat, finishing off his meal. She pursed her lips, perhaps wondering at the wisdom of ever having appointed this fellow. At length, he summoned a waiter and asked for his bill. When he'd paid, he said: "You told me that any interference in this man's work is unacceptable. Is this not so?"

"It is."

"And if his house was cracked, his wife violated, knives put to the throats of his babes until he was fleeced to the last penny – would that not have interfered?"

She was clearly unmoved by this argument, but, in no position to deny the truth, was forced to admit: "I imagine it would."

He shrugged into his greatcoat and pulled his gloves on. "The defence rests."

"I didn't ask for a bloodbath, captain."

"No, you asked for a soldier." He tapped the newspaper on the table. "And that's what you've got." And then he left.

41

VI

For three days he heard nothing more from Miss Evangeline, while his vigil was largely uneventful, though on the second night there was a brief curious incident.

It was shortly after midnight, and the Arctic temperatures were persisting. It hadn't snowed for a couple of days, but the sky was clear and the air so sharp that you fancied it would cut you. Sparrowhawk was at what he'd come to regard as his 'piquet point' behind the rhododendron bushes. It was concealed from the road, but gave him a clear view of the front of the property. Every so often he would walk around to the rear, but never saw any sign that the snow on the top of the garden wall or around its footings had been disturbed. On this particular occasion, he was in the park, walking back and forth, hugging himself, when again he had the feeling he was being watched. He spun around, ripping the Greener from its harness.

He'd have no compunction about opening fire. The incident with the Hoxton gang had shaken him slightly, but follow-up stories in the *London Illustrated News* had confirmed that the slain were a villainous band, who had kidnapped and outraged an innocent girl, the family of whom were more grateful to her anonymous rescuer than they could ever say. Mr. Cruikshank had added another caricature, depicting a dismal back street in which a terrifying figure, hooded and cowled like the Grim Reaper but leather gloved and clutching a firing-piece that looked alarmingly like Sparrowhawk's Greener, stood astride the bodies of several hooligans who had just been soundly thrashed. Underneath it, a caption read:

Monster, hero or both?

With no thought for such triviality now, Sparrowhawk advanced a few yards into the park. As always, the moonlight reflected brilliantly from the snow, and at first he saw nothing.

But then, gradually, he became aware of a heavy-set figure about thirty yards to the left of the bandstand. It stood perfectly still and watched him. He continued to advance, steadily. If this fellow was nothing more than a curious passer-by, the shotgun would involve some awkward explanations, but Sparrowhawk was playing for high stakes here, and he kept the weapon levelled.

A few yards more, however, and he relaxed again.

The figure was a snowman.

Some children must have built it during the day, though when he circled it, it struck him as being odder than usual. It had no features – no lumps of coal for eyes, no traditional carrot for a nose, yet someone had stuck a cigar where its mouth should be – a full-sized Cuban cheroot of the sort Sparrowhawk favoured but couldn't afford. Likewise, the evening coat and top-hat, the former of which was velvet, the latter silk, made for expensive adornments. Even though the figure had no eyes, he felt as though it was looking straight at him. He contemplated knocking the thing down and trampling it, but decided that this would be cruel on the children who'd built it. At the very least he could take the cheroot, though it occurred to him that maybe the cheroot had been left here specifically for that purpose and that it might have been tainted in some way. On reflection, that seemed a little ridiculous, though of course stranger things had so far happened.

He resumed his patrol, ignoring the snowman further. The rest of his shift was uneventful, and in the morning he went back to his residence. When he returned the following evening, he noticed that the snowman had gone. He wandered around, but there was no trace of it. There wasn't even a clump of messy snow where it had been standing. The surface was smooth, unbroken – even though there hadn't been another snow shower for a couple of days.

It was a puzzle, but he resolved to give no more thought to it. The vigil was becoming tedious, which meant that it was getting progressively easier for him to be distracted. As night fell

43

properly, and the streets again cleared of pedestrians, he tried not to dwell on the long hours that lay between now and the dawn. It was astonishing how lonely one could feel in a city as large as London in the depths of winter, though at roughly three o'clock the following morning, when he was almost comatose with cold and boredom, it became apparent that Sparrowhawk was very far from alone.

The first thing he noticed was the approaching jingle of bells. He thought he was dreaming and had to shake himself properly awake. But peering out through the rhododendrons, he beheld a bizarre figure prancing up the centre of Doughty Street. Initially, he thought his eyes were playing tricks, but then he remembered that it would soon be Christmas, and that maybe this was some form of fancy dress. The figure, which was slightly shorter than he was, wore large buckled shoes, bright green stockings, scarlet knee-length pantaloons, which were loose and bulky in the Jacobean style, a green doublet with a ruff collar, a scarlet chemise with puffed out sleeves, and green gloves. It carried a jester's marotte, which, as well as being woven with holly, was also hung with silver bells, and on its head wore a bright green cap, which was pointed but made of floppy material so that the bell on the end of it hung down. He couldn't quite see the figure's face, but it seemed to have a protruding nose and chin, with lush white whiskers down either cheek.

It capered up to Sparrowhawk's piquet point – and those were the only words he could use to describe its movements: 'prance', 'caper' – turned abruptly to its right, and continued to the gate of number 48, ringing its bells loudly, humming a ditty that sounded like *Ding Dong Merrily On High*.

Too bemused for caution, Sparrowhawk pushed through the rhododendrons and climbed over the railing.

"You there!" he said.

The elf – for that was the only way he could think of it – twirled around, gave a shrill squawk, and hared off northwards. Sparrowhawk chased after it. The elf was faster than he'd expected, though it ran awkwardly – it frolicked and gambolled, more like a puppet than a man – but he was able to track it by its piping laughter.

It led him a merry dance, veering along several streets at breakneck pace, never slipping or sliding whereas Sparrowhawk fell on every sharp turn, and finally waiting half way up Gray's Inn Road, where it jumped up and down, apparently cross that he hadn't been able to keep up with it. When it saw him stumble into view, it squealed delightedly and dashed down a narrow entry, at the end of which it crashed through a wall of foliage, which Sparrowhawk presumed belonged of the grounds of St. Pancras. Drawing his Greener, he went warily in after it, having to fight his way through masses of meshed and frozen twins, but suddenly emerging alongside a tall, stone-built property surrounded by a high wall.

He had thought he'd be ready for anything. But not this.

Any other person might have assumed it a groundskeeper's hut, or a gatehouse of some sort. However, it's similarity to 'the Parsonage', where Sparrowhawk had been born and raised, was undeniable. In fact, as he circled the property, that similarity became astounding, not to say impossible given that the real Parsonage was two hundred miles away at Kirkham, in Lancashire. He finally reached a pair of wrought-iron entrance gates – and yes, they were the same as those on the Parsonage, though clearly they hadn't been used for some time. They were not only closed and chained, but deep in dead and frosted vegetation. Their padlock was fused up with rust. Above them, he could see the central turret of the house, at the apex of which leaned a very old weathercock. This too was exactly the same as the one he'd known at home.

He continued to walk around the exterior until he encountered the narrow side-gate that he and his sister, Nan, had used as children. It was made of wood, but had rotted with age. Its lock hung off, so he pushed it open. On the other side lay what had once been the Parsonage's west lawn, though all he found now was deep, snow-covered bracken. He waded through it to a stone path, which he followed around to the front door. This stood half-open, icy blackness skulking on the other side.

Anyone else might have held back at this point, but Sparrowhawk was too perplexed to think straight. He entered a long, wood-panelled reception hall, which, though cloaked in near darkness, he could have walked blindfolded. A door stood open on the left. Through it, lay his father's old study. Glacial moonlight spilled into this, revealing shelves filled with dust and debris, a desk and floor strewn with torn books and dog-eared papers. Further along the hall, on the right, a door stood open on the old dining room. Sparrowhawk gazed through at a scene of equal desolation. It had once been decked for Christmas, but now evergreen trimmings hung desiccated from the overhead beams. Goblets and wine bottles lay shattered. Bowls of dates, figs and scented candles had once adorned the sideboards, but the candles had long ago dissolved and the fruit was nothing but mulch. On the central table, the festive feast was a malodorous shadow of its former self. Mice, cockroaches and other vermin scuttled amid the odious relics: a goose that was now carrion; steamed vegetables that were cobwebbed husks; an ornate Christmas cake thick with fungal fur. Strangely, there was no fetor, though the temperature might have accounted for that – the few intact panes in the window were rimed with frost both on the inside as well as the out.

Sparrowhawk strode on. Ahead of him, the door to the parlour was closed but, spotting a ruddy light around its edges, he pushed it open.

The room on the other side had always been the cosiest in the house. It looked through French windows onto a garden that in summer was a profusion of flowers and greenery. Its walls had been papered in pastel shades. It had always boasted comfortable furniture. Over the large mantelpiece there had once been an oil painting depicting his parents in their younger, more carefree days. Now the room was a shell: drab walls, bare boards on the floor, furniture shrouded with mildewed sheets. The ruddy light was cast by a few meagre coals glowing in the hearth, though these were sufficient to illuminate the elf figure, which waited for Sparrowhawk in the far corner, its arms raised above its head as if it was about to cast some fairy tale hex.

He approached it, frightened but at the same time fascinated.

The elf made no move, and when he got close he saw why. It wasn't a real man, but a marionette. It was life-size, but its face and hands were carved from jointed wood and had been crudely painted. Its body and limbs were suspended by strings, which rose towards the ceiling but were there lost in dimness. It was also – and this was perhaps the most disquieting thing of all – a close representation of his father.

It seemed that Doctor Joseph Sparrowhawk, the one-time academic, philosopher, publisher and pamphleteer – was now little more than a comic mannequin. Its head lay to one side; its eyes were glass baubles containing beads designed to roll crazily around. Its chin and nose were exaggerated – Punch-like, in the tradition of the season – but the lank white hair was the same, the white side-whiskers were the same, the prominent brow, the small, firm mouth.

Sparrowhawk prodded at it, wondering how he could have followed this effigy all the way from Doughty Street. It was solid, lifeless; it swayed where it hung.

Utterly confused but also feeling foolish and awkward, Sparrowhawk unbuttoned his greatcoat, and slid the Greener back into its harness – and realised that another figure was present. He only glimpsed it from the corner of his eye. It was seated to one side of the fire, where it had blended into the general dinginess of the room. He whirled around – and saw a woman. She wore a shawl and a plain, ordinary dress of the type favoured by his older sister, Nan. She was seated on a stool, but hunched forwards. Her hands were clasped on her lap, her eyes closed beneath her dust-rimmed bonnet.

"Nan?" he said. "Nan, is that … ?" He scuttled forwards and

crouched alongside her. The breath caught in his throat.

Nan was dead. Her skin had browned and wizened. It clung to the contours of her skull like dried tobacco leaves; it wrapped her clawed hands like shrivelled gloves.

"What in the name of … what is this?" he breathed, rising and backing away, only to be touched on the shoulder. Again, he spun around.

The marionette was directly behind him. Its arms were by its sides, but its head had jerked upright, the beads rolling in its bauble eyes. Its hinged jaw dropped to reveal a cavernous blood-red mouth, from which a demented squawk issued – the same squawk he had heard on Doughty Street. With stiff jerks of its strings, it again raised its arms. Then it raised its left leg, and brought it down hard. It did the same with its right, and suddenly it was dancing a wild, maniacal jig; at first in front of him, then to his right, and then to his rear. With piercing squeals of laughter, it cavorted around him like a dervish. Sparrowhawk stood rigid, closing his eyes, trying to shut out the horror. But the frenzied laughter grew in volume and shrillness until it was almost ear-shattering.

"Enough!" he finally roared.

He ripped out his sabre and, with three deft strokes, severed the dancing devil's strings. It crashed to the floor, again nothing more than a heap of lifeless, disjointed wood. But now a low sigh brought Sparrowhawk's attention back to his sister.

It was another stupefying shock to see that she was moving. Her dry, withered flesh seemed supple again. Her eyelids fluttered. Tears seeped onto her cheeks. Slowly, she began to weep – at first very softly, but with greater and greater passion, her shoulders soon heaving. She put a handkerchief to her face, but the tears soaked through it.

"Nan!" Sparrowhawk said, approaching. "Nan, it's me."

She shook her head. Her eyes were now open, but downcast, still overflowing.

"Nan …"

"I know it's you," she sobbed.

"Look at me, please."

"Why should I, after what you did?" He took her arm, but she yanked it free. "Such behaviour, John! And on Christmas Eve of all nights!

"Nan … that was eighteen years ago!"

"Father was never the same. The disappointment, the humiliation …"

"I won't be blamed for the humiliation. He started the fight, not I."

"But you were the one who played to the audience, John." Now she *did* turn her eyes on him, and they were fierce and cold and hostile. "What was it you said to him: 'You call yourself a freethinker, but in truth you're a puppet, an anarchist puppet!'"

"He spoke harshly to me as well."

"An 'anarchist puppet', John!" Her voice rose. "Think about that – after his life-long labours to ease the lot of the poor and helpless, you called your father 'a puppet!' – and in front of all his peers and contemporaries."

"I didn't know that every self-congratulating fraudster in the north of England would be here, did I!"

"'Self-congratulating fraudsters!'" Her eyes widened; she looked outraged. "John Sparrowhawk, how could you? Those were fine gentlemen – lawyers, writers."

"Radicals!" he retorted. "Trouble makers!"

"How dare you! Mr. Carlile – a true man of the people – had just been released from prison after long and unjust confinement. It was a great occasion. You too would have deemed it worth celebrating had you ever once seen further than your own interests."

He strode around the room, flustered. "Like I said, I didn't know father would have such august company."

"But you still picked your time, didn't you? You still chose to strike him on Christmas Eve, of all nights."

"Christmas Eve?" Sparrowhawk tried not to scoff. "When did

an avowed atheist like father ever darken a church door?"

"It was a family occasion. You knew there would be guests."

"It was the earliest opportunity I could get home."

"And then ..." She began to weep again. "And then to turn up in that ... that uniform."

"Nan, that was the dress-uniform of the 16th Light Dragoons. I'd been accepted for officer training. I'd hoped he would be proud."

"Proud? After all the speeches he made, all the pamphlets he issued?"

"I was his son, Nan, not his student. Nowhere was it written that I had to share his beliefs."

"He wanted you to go to the bar."

"What about what I wanted?"

She shook her head as if this was a familiar tale. "It was always about what *you* wanted, John ... with no thought for anyone else. Not even your family, let alone the great, suffering masses."

He turned his back on her, too angered to speak, but also too confused. It seemed that they'd had this conversation before, in this very room. Most likely it had been the morning following that dreadful Christmas Eve in 1825 – which surely made this sequel to it preposterous.

"But why do I bother?" Nan wept. "Why am I even talking to you?"

"Why are you even here?" he demanded, swinging around to face her – and seeing that she'd hunched forwards, and was stiff and withered again.

"Nan!" he shouted, hurrying over. "Nan, please ...!"

When he shook her, she swayed and rattled like bones wrapped in parchment. And then she collapsed, caving in on herself in a cloud of dust and decay.

"Nan!" he wailed, as the dried detritus of his sister spilled through his fingers. "Nan ... no!"

"Happy now?" a voice grated behind him.

He turned. As the corpse Nan had briefly become the real

Nan, now the puppet father had become the real father. Joseph Sparrowhawk stood before his son, looking as robust as he ever had, with his short but powerful frame, his flashing eyes, his flaring nostrils, his mouth trembling with emotion. Yet there were grotesque reminders of what he truly was: he still wore the ridiculous elf costume; metal hooks had been hammered into the backs of his hands, the sides of his knees, the toes of his feet, one even stood in the top of his head, and from these hook strands of severed puppet string still dangled. But the old man's aura was undeniable. Sparrowhawk felt as he always had when facing his father's wrath. The lank white hair, the ruddy cheeks puffing in and out, the stern brow furrowed with concentration – they awoke terrors in him that he'd thought long, long forgotten.

"Well sir?" the old man thundered. "Are you quite happy?"

"Father, I …"

"You see what you've brought on us?"

"I had my own life to lead …"

"And to ride roughshod over everyone else was the course it would take, and to hell with the world in the process!" As always with his father, it was a statement rather than a question. "To hell in a hand-basket with the whole wretched world, just as long as you got your own way!"

Sparrowhawk shook his head. "Father, you don't … you *can't* believe that?"

"Telling me what I believe now, boy?"

"Father, this is madness. You can't be here. This house can't be…"

"Reality won't change just because you want it to!" The old man's voice rose to a furious pitch. His ruddy cheeks became crimson. Froth spurted onto his lips. "You wretch! You reprobate! It's high time you were dealt with, boy … and it's my curse to be the one who must do it!"

"Father please, listen to me … I know this seems like an excuse. I didn't mean to cause as much hurt. I know you were offended. But father, I just wanted to do what the other chaps at

51

school were doing."

The old man wasn't listening. He wandered across the room, still with that crazy, puppet gait, and started rummaging along shelves filled with rot and foulness.

"I became a war hero for God's sake!" his son protested. "Doesn't that count for anything?"

"It might, if God existed." The old man turned back around. He'd found what he was looking for – a willow cane with a curved handle, which he was now flexing between his crippled hands. "But he doesn't, and neither do you ... to *me*, John Sparrowhawk. So here's what you deserve."

The first few blows startled Sparrowhawk rather than hurt him. But they were hard, stinging slashes across his face, and across his hands when he raised them to protect himself.

"Father stop this! Don't be ridiculous! Father this won't make any difference." The blows continued, across Sparrowhawk's body as well as his arms and head. The ferocity of the attack grew, each impact a deafening *thwack*. "Look, you old fool ... I was flogged a hundred times at school. You think your paltry efforts can ..."

But his words petered out when he saw the look on his father's face.

It was bestial, twisted with rage. Beads of sweat stood on the florid brow. Spittle seethed between the old man's lips as he slashed and slashed with the cane. For a second or two the pain meant nothing to Sparrowhawk, so stunned was he by this vision. He even dropped his guard, and took several more blows, clean and unobstructed, across his face.

Joseph Sparrowhawk had always been a domineering man: caustic, acid-tongued, an intellectual bully who would browbeat those seeking to dispute with him. But he was not violent. In fact, he abhorred and opposed violence in every form, and always had.

The cane whistled down again, but this time Sparrowhawk caught it in his gloved fist. "You never flogged me before," he said, peering into the deranged eyes. "Not once. You've never believed in corporal punishment. *You're not my father at all!*'

The old man's purple face split into a leering grin. Instead of trying to yank the cane free, he twisted its curved handle. There was a *click* and, with a gleam of metal, he pulled a swordstick from it.

"Too late for that," Sparrowhawk said, backing away. "You bloody impostor!"

The old man lunged with his blade, but Sparrowhawk had now drawn his own. He fended the swordstick easily and with such force that it went clattering to the ground, and then clutched his enemy by the throat. The old man flailed, giving more demented squawks. From somewhere behind him, Sparrowhawk heard the shrieks of his corpse-sister. Female fists beating futilely on his back – but it wasn't Nan and this wasn't his father. He now knew that for certain. The temptation was to drive his sabre home, once, twice, as many times as it took – but no, that was not the victory he was seeking here. Instead, he pushed his opponent steadily backwards.

"You are not my father!" he said again. "But I don't need to kill the likes of you in order to beat you."

The puppet horror – for that was the shape it had resumed – continued to writhe, its eyes sightless, its wooden jaws clacking together. Sparrowhawk forced it backwards until they blundered into the heavy curtain beside the French window, which collapsed on them in a heap, tangling them in dust and rotting material. Sparrowhawk lost his grip on the puppet. He hacked angrily around with his sabre, trying to cut himself free – only to discover that he was actually hacking at undergrowth, at rhododendron bushes.

Abruptly, he realised that there was snow under his feet, and that overhead a cool, blue dawn was flushing the London sky. Beyond the railings and across the road, 48, Doughty Street was coming to life. He saw candlelight in its windows, and silhouettes moving around. He fancied he heard the laughing voices of children. A carriage trundled past, spurting snow from its wheels.

Clearly, he hadn't slept and dreamed the whole thing – his face and hands were covered with livid welts. But this only made it a hundred times worse. Confused and dismayed, he tottered back across the park to where Peppercorn was waiting. The animal nuzzled him warmly when he reached it, breathing its steamy breath all over him. He'd never been as glad to see a friend in his life.

VII

As usual, after a long night's watch, Sparrowhawk took to his bed straight away, but on this occasion sleep eluded him.

Eventually, just before noon, he walked back to Doughty Street, to see if he'd left any tracks from the previous night, and if it was possible to follow them back to the ruined manse that he'd fancied was his childhood home. But it was a lovely winter's day, and there was much traffic around, both pedestrian and vehicular, and any trail he may have left had long been obliterated. He moved back behind the rhododendrons, and stared across the road. For the first time, he saw the man that he was here to protect; a slim, youngish gentleman, not particularly imposing but very stylishly dressed. He had a pretty woman on his arm, presumably his wife, and four young children waddling around him like geese, two girls and two boys. He and his family left the house just after eleven o'clock, climbed into a carriage and headed off into the snow-clad city. They seemed very happy together, which, for some reason – probably his own innate loneliness – cut Sparrowhawk to the quick.

When he noticed a fragrance of rose and jasmine, he turned and found Miss Evangeline at his shoulder. She was pert and handsome as ever, wearing a blue velvet cloak over her chequered dress, and a fetching beribboned bonnet.

"You told me the chap in the carriage was the intended target," Sparrowhawk said.

"So he is."

"Well last night the target was evidently me."

"Of course. You are now his protector, his guardian. To get to him, they must first get through you. They know that, and they are acting accordingly."

Sparrowhawk sighed. "Who are 'they'?"

"That's not a question I can answer yet but, as I told you before, there are three of them in total. The first of them you have already seen off. I realise it was quite a test for you, but you didn't fail."

As always with Miss Evangeline, it came as no surprise to him that she seemed to know everything that had happened.

"Is it going to be like this each time?" he asked.

"I told you they were clever. Did you think we'd go to the expense of recruiting you if our foe was a mere bunch of thieves and kidnappers?"

"You talk in cryptic riddles." He started walking, unconcerned whether she could keep up with his long stride – though, predictably, she had no problem. "I don't know if I can finish this work."

"You're already a third of the way through it," she said.

"You say there will be two more visitants?"

"That is our estimation."

"How do you know that exactly?"

"We have our sources."

"Well don't bother telling me. I'm only the one in the firing line."

"We hired a soldier, captain, as you are fond of pointing out. Isn't 'being in the firing line' part of the job?"

They reached the park gates, where Miss Evangeline's black enamel coach was waiting, the driver as patient and still as ever and, as before, wrapped so heavily against the chill that his face was invisible.

"Are you leaving already?" Sparrowhawk asked, suddenly weary of being alone.

"Don't you wish to go home and sleep?" she said.

"Not yet. Can we walk together for a little while? I need some fresh air."

"And how can I help with that?"

"You can't. But you're an extremely beautiful woman, and I'd be proud to have you with me."

She pondered this, then signalled her coachman to leave them. He whipped his horses away, and she and Sparrowhawk began to stroll, arm in arm.

"I should warn you now, captain," she said. "You and I can never be together."

"Is that a challenge?"

"No, it's a fact."

"What if I was to say that I've fallen in love with you?"

"I would not believe it. You barely know me, and you are a man of the world not a child."

"Very well. What if I was to admit that I don't love you, but that I would very much like to take you to bed?"

"I would be offended."

"No you wouldn't. You're as much a woman of the world as I'm a man of the world."

"Then I would spare you the pain of entertaining hopes that can never be fulfilled."

"I might use underhand tactics, miss. I could claim to be so distraught by what happened last night that I need a soft breast to lay my head against before I can continue the vigil."

"Again, you would be lying. We chose you because you are not the sort of person to be left distraught by anything."

"Would it be so unthinkable, you and I? Is it so foul a thought to you?"

He glanced sidelong, interested to see her response. She was studied, thoughtful.

"In itself, no," she eventually said. "But it would distract us from the business at hand, and that can not be allowed."

"And when this business is over?"

"Why run before our horses to market?"

"A man must have something to cling onto."

"You will have plenty to cling onto in due course."

"No matter." He tried not to sound too grumpy. "I ask for companionship, nothing more."

"If it's merely companionship you seek …"

"Must I spell it out? I need to talk. Anyone will do, though preferably I'd like to talk with someone who understands my predicament."

She nodded, accepting this. They were now headed through Holborn, which was thronging with shoppers. It was still a couple of working weeks off the Christmas holiday, but London's retailers were getting in the mood. The poulterers' windows were filled with hanging fowl and fat, fleshy turkeys. In the butchers, there were strings of sausages and choice cuts of pork and beef. Market stalls were bundled with ivy, holly and mistletoe.

"In his younger days, my father was a devotee of Tom Paine," Sparrowhawk said. "*The Rights Of Man* was his Bible. He shared Paine's enthusiasm for the revolutions in America and France. He never accepted that the latter was more of a holocaust than a triumph. During the war against Napoleon, he insisted to the very end that we were fighting on the wrong side."

Miss Evangeline said nothing. They continued to walk.

"I suppose it's not difficult to see why he held these views. Father was always a moral man, and we, being an old Lancashire family, saw for ourselves what happened when the rural poor were lured into industry. Initially, the new jobs in the towns looked promising to them, with better wages and purpose-built dwellings on which the rent was low. Of course, the workers never knew until it was too late that wages would only be paid in coins specially issued by the mine and mill owners, which could only be spent in the mine and mill shops, where goods were sparse and expensive, and that their low-rent dwellings were low-rent because they were damp, draughty and riddled with vermin – and because they were right in the midst of fire, smoke and chaos on an infernal scale. The Parsonage was built on a high moor, but from my bedroom window you could see the blackened plain below, bristling with chimneys and pit-wheels. The sky over it was a permanent pall of smoke. Peterloo, I think, compounded father's views. He was there in person. Nan was with him. You remember the massacre of Peterloo?"

"I know of it," she said. "I wasn't there, of course."

"I wasn't there either. I was too young, not even ten years old."

Sparrowhawk thought again about the appalling incident in question. It was back in 1819, when an enormous but peaceful crowd of weavers and other cotton-folk had gathered on Peter's Field in Manchester, to hear the speaker, Henry Hunt, make a call for universal suffrage. That call never came, because no sooner had the meeting commenced than two squadrons of mounted cavalry rode into the midst of the crowd in an attempt to arrest Hunt and his associates. Many of the demonstrators linked arms to try and prevent this, but the troops cut their way through, slashing at heads and arms, urging their horses on, knocking people flat, men, women and children alike. When it was obvious the first detachment wasn't going to reach the podium, a second detachment – a further two squadrons of horse – were also sent in, these under strict orders to clear the field. This they did, at horrendous cost to the unarmed crowd, who, even though many among them were now maimed and dying, were mercilessly ridden down. At the end of the day, eleven lay dead and a further five hundred were horribly injured.

Though he'd only heard about it in hearsay, Peterloo had always struck a resonance with Sparrowhawk because, though born of a different class, he had grown up side-by-side with that toiling workforce, those blackers and stokers, those colliers and loom-workers. Through his father's insistence, he'd been *made* to know them, to sympathise with them, to fraternise with their young – which was easy enough when you yourself were young, because what do children see in a child except another child? So, as a boy, he'd played with them on perfectly equal terms, romping over the great humps of slag where once there'd been moor and coppice; chasing back and forth along the cinder tow-paths, through the brick tunnels, along the lonely mineral-lines where ponies hauled colossal tubs of coal. He still remembered his companions' names and faces: Benjamin Burrows, with the red hair and freckles; Tom Chadwick, who had jet-black curls but a nasty lisp; Martin Dawson, reed-thin and sensitive, always kind to animals; Betty Gornall, willowy and fair-haired – she would probably go on to break a hundred hearts. One of them – he wasn't sure which, as Nan had refused to tell him – had lain among the trampled and torn on Peter's Field.

It wasn't difficult to picture such carnage, for Sparrowhawk had seen the results of cavalry charges many times since; the bodies smashed by iron-shod hooves, the fantastically re-arranged limbs, the slashed faces and cloven skulls, the deepening scarlet streams in the mire of mud and pulverised flesh.

"Anyone of conscience might have turned radical under those circumstances," he muttered, surprising himself with such a viewpoint.

"And would that be so bad a thing?" Miss Evangeline asked.

"Even the best principles can be taken too far. For my thirteenth birthday, which I spent at school, father sent me a copy of Godwin's tome on political science."

"And is that not a great work of social and political thought?"

"Yes, but it was also thirty years out of date and highly contentious. Godwin spent most of his later life in hiding – even his fellow egalitarians thought him a lunatic. When the chaps at school saw it, they made sport of me for days. Then the humour dried up – they took note of my Lancashire accent, and started putting two and two together. They became suspicious, started calling me 'the agitator', 'the enemy'. Even some of the masters felt the same. I had to work twice as hard just to win back my basic self-respect. Being good was no longer enough. Now I had to be the best just to be accepted: best in class, best in the exam hall, best runner, best rugby player, best boxer. I had to be best boy in every shape and form."

"So, in an indirect way," Miss Evangeline said, "you owe your father everything."

"That's true. Though 'everything' hasn't turned out to be very much in my case. As my current bondage attests."

By this time they were on Newgate Street, and were swept up by the crowds flocking into Old Bailey Lane to watch the hanging of James Keggs, the so-called 'Beast of Bermondsey'. Despite the intense cold, the mob was in full strength and voice, all classes and creeds represented, the coster folk eagerly supplying them with wintry consumables, everything from boiled puddings to roast chestnuts and hot coffee. Excitable urchins darted back and forth; occasionally a beadle or constable managed to get hold of one and whipped him until he yowled, before kicking him on his way. A tall placard in the midst of the crowd revealed the presence of a long-song seller. "Three yards a yenep, three a yenep!" he shouted hoarsely, as he told the ghoulish tale of James Keggs, a buckle-maker from Southwark, who had lured four unfortunate women back to his cellar room, and there throttled them and raped their corpses. Several well-to-do ladies did the honourable thing by fainting in their carriages.

"Four victims," Miss Evangeline said. "That's two short of your tally."

"Hardly," Sparrowhawk replied. "My full tally would make your toes curl."

At ground level, there was more mirth about the murders than disgust. Fully grown men clawed their hands or pulled taut their neckerchiefs as, howling like banshees, they prepared to jump upon gap-toothed harridans, who cackled drunkenly. One portly fellow – a dustman by his fantail cap – lay facedown and mimicked making love to a plank of wood, to even wilder guffaws. It was a nightmarish scene. The snow had now been churned to filthy mush; there was a nauseating reek of sewage. Looming over everything, Newgate Prison looked even grimmer than usual. Its massive, black brick walls were streaked with sickly, greenish ice; similar greenish spears dangled from its eaves.

Just before two o'clock, the prison bell began to toll, and Keggs was brought through the Debtor's Door, his arms pinioned by rope. A prison warder stood to either side of him, while the prison chaplain walked behind, intoning without interest.

When they beheld the 'Beast', the crowd tooted and whistled – and the cordon of mounted constables keeping them separate

61

from the gallows became uneasy. The condemned was not the monster everyone had been expecting, but a fellow of small, thin stature, barefoot and clad in prison greys that were too big for him. He was dirty and badly bruised.

He struggled violently and gibbered for mercy as he was wrestled onto the trapdoor. Up close, for Sparrowhawk and Miss Evangeline had managed to get a good position, Keggs was rather simple looking, with a low-slung brow, buckteeth and jug ears. He croaked in despair, his terrified eyes flirting left and right as the white hood was pulled down over his head. The executioner fixed the noose in place and, as the tolling bell ceased, stepped back and pulled the lever. The baying of the mob rose to a crescendo as the trapdoor swung down and the prisoner dropped. He tilted sideways as he descended, smashing his face against the edge of the trap, before spinning down to the end of the rope and jerking to a halt – he twisted and gurgled for several minutes, the front of his white hood turning slowly crimson, but eventually hung still.

Very quickly after that – remarkably quickly in fact, and in eerily orderly fashion – the spectators dispersed, drifting away in ones and twos. A short while later, the black flag was raised above the prison wall. Keggs would remain where he was, turning in the icy breeze, guarded by the warders and the constables for at least another hour. But there would be no sequel. It was over.

"Your father railed against spectacles like this, did he not?" Miss Evangeline said.

Sparrowhawk, who'd been grim and silent throughout the execution, nodded. "And yet he conveniently forgot the much more frequent use of the guillotine in Revolutionary France."

"Just because he wouldn't talk about those atrocities in France, does that mean he denied they ever happened?"

"I think he was disappointed by the way the revolutionaries also became tyrants. It's interesting … there was a lively debate at the hustings during the Whigs' 1820 election campaign, and I heard him lose out to a country clergyman. Father was deriding the Christian Church for allowing its ideals to be corrupted, saying that because of this it was flawed as an institution and that its adherents were deluded fools and scallywags. The clergyman replied by asking if father's thesis also applied to the corruption of the revolutionary ideals that led to the Terror and the rise of Bonapartism, and wondered if that meant the dogma of radicalism was equally flawed and if those who followed that creed were equally a bunch of deluded fools and scallywags. For the first time in his life, father was lost for words. It was like a new concept he couldn't grapple with. Oh yes, he was a libertarian but make no mistake, he could be a brute in his way. Those who defied him were often rewarded cruelly. My joining the army offended his beliefs, and he never, ever forgave me. He didn't even reply to the invitation to my wedding. Nan did, but only with a polite card. But I suppose if father had lived longer, age might have mellowed him."

"If he'd lived longer?" Miss Evangeline sounded surprised. "But he's still alive."

They'd begun to walk again, but now came to an abrupt standstill.

"Father is alive?" Sparrowhawk said, astonished.

She nodded, and smiled brightly.

"And Nan?"

"She's alive too. Your father is old and infirm, admittedly, but they still live at the Parsonage, where your sister nurses him. Despite your father's age, they are both active in the Chartist movement."

"But …" Sparrowhawk was almost lost for words. "But last night…"

"Phantasms, captain. As I thought you'd realised."

Sparrowhawk's legs suddenly felt weak. He was aware of the blood running from his face, leaving his pallor ashen. "Of all …" he stammered. "Of all the tricks you have played so far, miss, this is the lowest."

"Forgive me, if I misled you …"

63

"Misled me! Is this sport for you? Some kind of elaborate diversion? I may be nothing more in you and your employers' eyes than a lump of hired muscle, a battle-scarred thug who can be relied on to brutalise any foe at the drop of a hat. But I have feelings too, you know. I can be hurt."

"Now, Captain Sparrowhawk, you surely can't think I would…"

"Enough. It ill becomes any gentleman to leave a lady without a chaperone at a hanging, but that is exactly what I am going to do. Good day, Miss Evangeline."

And he strode quickly away.

VIII

Sparrowhawk returned to his lodgings that afternoon, to find that an envelope had been delivered. It was addressed simply to 'Captain John Sparrowhawk', which meant that it had been delivered by hand. He went back into the courtyard, looking around, but only one or two of his fellow residents were abroad, and none of them paid him any heed. When he opened the envelope, it contained a black card printed with gold characters, and invited him as "the esteemed Cpt. Sparrowhawk" to an annual Christmas banquet, which would be hosted by General George Pollock at the Officers' Club on Cooper's Row, Tower Hill. The time was eight o'clock in the evening, on December 11th.

Sparrowhawk made up the fire, and sat in the easy chair to consider it.

General Pollock was a legend, an artilleryman who had risen through the ranks, and a 'human thunderbolt' as Sparrowhawk had heard him described while a cadet at the Royal Military College, Sandhurst. A hero of the battles of Deig and Bhurporte, of the Nepal War and the Burmese Campaigns, Pollock was said to be more like a lion than a man, stern of brow and fiery of temper, but also an astute tactician, a leader from the front and an inspirer of his troops, who would follow him to Hell if necessary. Hadn't Miss Evangeline said that it was Pollock who'd avenged the disaster at Kabul by massacring the Ghilazi tribe and sundry other recalcitrant Afghans? That would be in keeping with the mythology woven around him.

Under normal circumstances, to receive a personal invitation of this sort would be a great honour. The mere presence of General Pollock in London was something that most military men, or former military men, could not ignore. But Sparrowhawk's position was far from simple. After the revolting trick played on him the previous night, he no longer felt any loyalty to Miss Evangeline and her party, but he'd given his word that he'd keep vigil every night until December 21st. His word was not as binding as a contract, but he still didn't like to break it.

He paced his rooms.

Christmas dinner with General Pollock.

Sparrowhawk imagined the possibilities. Pollock, being a soldier's soldier, was not the sort to be impressed by those pink, pompous dandies who peppered the lecture halls at Sandhurst. He'd prefer fighting men, men who'd won deserved accolades in the face of the enemy. He wouldn't be upset to hear rural or urban accents among his officers; he'd be more concerned with how they performed under fire, how they stood their ground, how they motivated their troops. Perhaps this was the reason behind the invitation? Pollock would be very familiar with the events that occurred in Afghanistan before he was sent there to quell the uprising. If he'd heard how Sparrowhawk had performed, contesting every yard of ground, losing his entire command in the process and being desperately wounded himself, would the general not then have been horrified to hear how Sparrowhawk's reckless but grief-stricken decision to resign his commission had landed him in the debtors' gaol, when most of those debts had been incurred by his estate having to pay doctors to tend his ailing wife? Would the general not have been even more horrified, not to say totally outraged, to hear how the army, fuelled by a school of thought that, while it might have paid lip-service to Sparrowhawk's heroism by approving his medals and his mentions in despatches, had always mistrusted and even resented officers who spoke and behaved like commoners, and thus had piously abandoned him to his terrible fate?

It seemed unlikely, but could *this* be Sparrowhawk's recompense? It would be a shamefully belated recompense admittedly, but anything was better than nothing. He'd certainly be a fool to turn such an opportunity down. He'd never serve in the Colours again, but to have a friend like General Pollock could be invaluable. Once Sparrowhawk's work for Miss Evangeline was completed, what would he do? Return to Soho's drinking dens and gambling rooms? Perhaps this time next year he'd be back in the Fleet, or maybe somewhere even worse. He'd heard a whisper that the Fleet was closing, and that the disease-ridden King's Bench Prison, already crammed to its walls with manacled felons, would be the next destination for London's debtors.

He pondered the problem all the following night while he stood guard on Doughty Street. There were no disturbances to distract him, except that the temperature fell even further (the icy grip of winter was tightening inexorably – stories were rife that, all over the city, vagrants were actively seeking the shelter of the workhouse rather than fleeing from it). The next morning, when he returned to Camden Town, he still hadn't made a decision. The way Sparrowhawk saw it, to attend General Pollock's banquet would only mean that he'd need to abscond from his duty for one night. It was entirely possible that this might be the night of the second visitation to Doughty Street, but that was a risk he could alleviate a little. Once he'd slept that afternoon, he rose, dressed in his working garb and set off on foot.

On the south bank of the Thames, just opposite the Tower, a minor river called the Neckinger, which wound its way through the worst sewers and filthiest ditches in Bermondsey and Southwark, discharged itself in the form of two separate streams, which diverged about a hundred yards back from the Thames' edge, creating a small and slimy atoll known locally as Jacob's Island. These two streams were the colour of green tea, and thick, not just with human waste, but with the vile outpourings of every factory, workshop, tannery shed, slaughterhouse, kennel and septic tank in London's woe-begotten southern neighbourhoods – so rich were they in steaming effluent that even at this time of year they didn't freeze over. To make things worse, in severe weather they could each swell to perhaps thirty feet in breadth, providing a loathsome barrier, which had become known as 'Folly Ditch' because one could only attempt to cross it via rotten pilings laid across loose bricks. The rat-infested buildings on the island were equally repulsive: a clutch of old tenements partially sunken into the mud. They leaned precariously against each other, and were so streaked with dirt, soot and the faeces of gulls and pigeons that just to look at them might knock a normal person sick. Every window in them was broken and boarded, every doorway lop-sided or cluttered with foul refuse. Great fissures snaked through their crazy brickwork, while countless slates had fallen from their roofs, leaving naked joists. Yet almost incredibly, a tavern was sandwiched between these crumbling edifices, which was still in business.

It was called *The Moon O'er The Mire*, and it was in here where Sparrowhawk located Daniel Willoughby, formerly Trooper Willoughby of the 16th Light Dragoons.

The Afghan War had not been kind to Willoughby, in particular the battle at Ghuznee, where he'd been caught in a storm of grapeshot, which had torn his face asunder and smashed his left leg to pulp. Somehow he'd survived, though his life now was more akin to a living death. Sparrowhawk found him seated in a hearthside nook, masked from the tavern entrance by a riotous horde of ruffians and doxies. He was grizzled, bristled, and painfully thin, wrapped in a patched up greatcoat and, rather incongruously, wearing an old Napoleonic bicorne. He sported an eye-patch on the right hand side, though it did little to conceal his grisly facial scars, and a timber shaft where his left leg had once been. Sparrowhawk placed a mug of gin in front of him, before sitting at the small table.

At first Willoughby looked baffled and hostile. But then his grotesque features split into a toothless grin.

"Why Mr. Sparrer-awk, sir … how long has it been?"

"Too long, Dan."

"How's yourself, sir?"

"I've had a hard time, Dan, though not as hard, I fear, as you."

Willoughby shrugged. "No-one wants a broken old soldier, do they, sir? When the fighting's done, what use are we?"

"I may have a use for you, Dan?"

"How's that, sir?"

"I can pay you too."

Willoughby looked wary. "I can always use money, sir. Though what good I'll be to you, I don't know. There isn't much I can do in the way of work."

"Can you still fire a weapon, Dan?"

"I can, sir." Willoughby chuckled and tapped his eye-patch. "If you want me to hit the side of the Tower of London, that is."

"I'll let you have use of my Greener. It's difficult to miss any target with that."

Willoughby looked shocked. "Your own Greener shotgun, sir?"

"That's the one. It's like a piece of hand-artillery."

"That was a fine weapon, sir. If I recall, you purchased it at your own expense. You sure you want to part with it? Even for a short time?"

"I think it may be necessary for your safety, Dan?"

"I'd certainly feel safe with a weapon like that at my side, sir." Willoughby mused. "My my, your old Greener. The gunsmiths of Newcastle knew their trade, and no mistake. Mind you, sir, I don't even know what it is you want me to do yet."

"Hopefully you won't have to do much." Sparrowhawk fingered his own mug – it contained a single shot of rum. "Except watch a house for one night. There's five pounds for you, if you can do that."

"Five… ?" Willoughby's single eye bulged like a duck egg. His lacerated cheeks paled. "Five whole pounds, sir?"

"Five pounds. Two of them as a commission up front, the rest on completion of the work. But I warn you, Dan, I'll feel bad if all you do is drink that money away."

"Oh no, sir, of course not, sir. That much will get me a warm bed for a few nights and, I dare say, will put some hot food in my belly."

"You'll need to be sobre on the night in question, which is December 11th. That's a week from now."

"I'll be s-sobre, sir." Willoughby stammered. He was almost

breathless with joy. "You mark my words."

"All right. I'll collect you at five o'clock in the evening, on the 11th. Where can I meet you, Dan?"

"Right here, sir."

Sparrowhawk regarded him dubiously.

"Don't be fooled by appearances, Mr. Sparrer-awk, sir." Willoughby gave a rasping chuckle. "I'm only really in here for the warmth of all these bodies. You'd be surprised how long I can make a gill of gin last. Six hours and forty minutes is my record so far."

"That's impressive, Dan." Sparrowhawk finished his rum and stood up. "But there's one other thing. Do you happen to have your old canteen on you?"

"Of course, sir." Willoughby rummaged in his kit bag, to a clatter of cutlery and mess tins. "Everything I own is in here."

"You won't need it now, Dan." Sparrowhawk moved towards the entrance. "Just make sure you have it on the 11th. It could be a long night."

VIX

Nothing unusual happened at Doughty Street for the next few days. One morning, shortly before Sparrowhawk was due to go off duty, he saw the fellow he was guarding leave the premises with a pile of documents under his arm and take a carriage. He was tense and appeared to be in a rush; as the coachman whipped the team away, Sparrowhawk saw the passenger take a pencil from under his lapel and make rapid alterations to his paperwork.

Curious, Sparrowhawk mounted Peppercorn and followed. This was not easy given that the snowy streets were now bustling, however it was not a long journey – down through Covent Garden and across Trafalgar Square, where the new column of Lord Nelson was in the process of being erected, to a narrow passage off Piccadilly. Here, the man hurried into a nondescript building through a tradesman's door, which slammed closed behind him. He was in no apparent rush to reappear, and it became clear to Sparrowhawk that hanging around outside would be impossible if he wished to remain inconspicuous. He thus headed back to Camden Town, content that he would learn everything in due course.

Later that day, when he'd risen from his bed, he bought some papers, a quill and an inkpot. For the two hours before he went back on watch, he agonised over whether or not to write a letter to his father and sister. Eventually he decided against it. He told himself that this was because he had important work to attend, and that he couldn't afford any interruptions to his schedule. Though in reality – and he silently cursed himself when he realised this – it was because he didn't have the first idea how to word such an epistle. What was he supposed to do? Offer a heartfelt apology? Demand an apology from them? Brag about his Afghan exploits in an effort to win admiration? Tell them his tale of woe to try and elicit sympathy? None felt appropriate, and neither, if he was honest, did putting his thoughts on paper when a more decent option would be to visit them in person, which in itself was not a pleasant notion and was something he was glad to put off for the time being.

X

December 11th was the coldest day thus far.
Snow hadn't fallen for several days – on December 9th it
had even rained for an hour, but this had not signalled a thaw.
With the ground frozen solid and the air temperature so low, the
rain had compressed the lying snow and formed a layer of ice on
top of it, making for exceedingly treacherous footing. On the
night of December 10th, the thermometers fell lower than anyone
in England could remember. In the North Country, they touched
twenty degrees below freezing. In London they were somewhat
more benign – at fifteen degrees below, and this did not improve
as the 11th dawned. The sun rose briefly over the horizon – a
glacial jewel in a sky that was more like a bed of ash, and shed not
an ounce of warmth on the frostbitten city. When darkness
returned in late afternoon, the temperatures plunged even lower.

Daniel Willoughby, as he'd promised, was waiting at the *Moon
O'er The Mire* when Sparrowhawk arrived. With the alleys and
footways like skating rings, it was clear that Willoughby, with his
peg-leg, was going to have trouble walking any distance let alone
as far as Bloomsbury. Sparrowhawk opted to carry him on his
back, at least to London Bridge, where they could collect a
hackney coach. There were hoots and sniggers from several
passers-by, but Sparrowhawk was not embarrassed. Many times
in the past, he'd carried wounded comrades on his back. It
occurred to him more than once before they reached London
Bridge that a man who could barely stand up in these conditions
was not likely to be a useful ally, but he shook such fears from his
head. After all, this was the night of General Pollock's banquet.

En route to Bloomsbury, he paid Willoughby the initial fee,
and told him as much as he needed to know about the operation
– which, in truth, was about as much as Sparrowhawk knew –
then handed him the shotgun and an adequate supply of
cartridges, insisting that he keep these concealed under his
greatcoat. He also provided food and drink for his temporary

73

replacement, and gave an assurance that he would be there to take over in the early hours of the morning.

When he installed Willoughby behind the rhododendrons, he noticed how deeply the peg-leg sank through the crust of snow, and again he had reservations. But it would be an extreme neglect of duty to leave 48, Doughty Street unguarded even for a short time during the hours of darkness. The die, Sparrowhawk decided, had been cast.

On returning to Camden Town, he spent half an hour getting ready for the great event. He no longer boasted a dress-uniform of course, or any of his medals, but attired himself in the best garments that Miss Evangeline and her people had provided: a frilled shirt, a brightly flowered waistcoat, a large blue blow-tie and a blue evening coat with gilt buttons. He threw on his greatcoat, donned his topper at a rakish angle, and rode to Cooper's Row in some style, he felt.

On arrival, he entered a large courtyard lit by flaring torches, where Hapsburgian footmen in powdered wigs, white stockings and buckled shoes, rushed about, taking charge of animals and carriages, and ushering the various guests through a large entrance with an ornate griffin – or some such heraldic creature – perched on its snow-clad lintel. In an anteroom filled with eastern prints and lush, exotic plants, numerous young officers modelled a variety of handsome uniforms: pressed blue and scarlet tunics, embroidered pelisses, gold and silver braid, white trims, white piping – all milling together enthusiastically, comparing their experiences at the tops of their voices. Sparrowhawk saw representatives from the Norfolk Foot, the Royal Anglians, the Somerset Light Infantry, the East Surrey Foot, the Princess of Wales's Regiment – but nowhere could he find a colleague from the 16th Light Dragoons, which puzzled and disappointed him more than he'd expected.

All newcomers were checked on a list before being issued with a seating card and given the option of sherry or champagne, of which Sparrowhawk chose the latter and was subsequently treated to several flutes. When the assembly was complete, a bagpiper played them through an arched, whitewashed tunnel into a great, candle-lit eating hall. At one end there was a roaring fire, its mantel decked with Christmas brocade, though the bulk of the décor in the room was military, comprising countless emblems and battle standards, both home-grown and captured on the field. The dining tables were arranged around the edges of the hall, aside from the head-table, where the banquet's host and his special guests would be seated. Down the centre, a very long table groaned beneath the weight of a festive feast. Every type of culinary luxury was on display: roast turkeys stuffed with figs and hazelnuts, saddles of pork glazed with sweet sauce, platters of salmon garnished with oysters, roast duckling, roast quail, beef and ale pies, chicken pies, mutton pies, venison pies, lamb shanks, trays of German sausage, bowls of steamed and minted vegetables. There were also cakes, puddings, tarts, plates of biscuits and great wedges of cheese filled with cranberries, apricots and other rich, spiced fruit.

When General Pollock appeared, there were roars of appreciation. He was every inch the figure of legend: a great, bluff, hearty fellow, broad of shoulder, barrel of chest, and sparkling in his artilleryman's dress-uniform of cocked hat and blue tunic with its scarlet collar, gold cord loops and white belt. His hair was an immense, tawny mane, which extended onto his cheeks and top lip in the largest pair of mutton-chop whiskers Sparrowhawk had ever seen. When he greeted each guest personally, his grip was strong, almost overpowering. His large, penetrating eyes were as gold as sunburned savannah grass. Yet, when he came face-to-face with Sparrowhawk, having initially looked dismayed to see civilian garb, he broke into the warmest and toothiest of smiles.

"Captain Sparrowhawk!" he boomed.

Sparrowhawk clicked his heels and bowed slightly. It didn't feel right to make a formal salute when he was no longer in the service. "I'm honoured, my lord. And exceedingly grateful for your invitation."

"The honour is mine, captain. You'll note from our seating arrangements that you've been placed alongside me at the head-table?"

Sparrowhawk was astounded, and said so.

"Not a bit of it, dear chap," General Pollock replied. "There'll always be room at my table for heroes of a genuine ilk."

When the meal commenced, it was a military banquet in the old sense in that it was almost disorderly. Grace was hurried, and footmen ran breathlessly back and forth as they served food and drink to the diners, scampering in and out of the kitchen doors to replenish the rapidly dwindling stocks. Bottle after bottle of wine was consumed, dish after dish was polished off. The general ate with monstrous gusto, grabbing up a huge turkey leg, and tearing at it with his ivory teeth. From some unseen place in the room, musicians provided a succession of overtures, both seasonal and military. The conversation rose frequently to such an intense level of noise that it was difficult to imagine anyone hearing anyone else. Sparrowhawk, who found the atmosphere heady and at times dream-like, was struck with the bizarre illusion of a room filled with seated dogs, all barking insanely at each other.

When the meal was complete, trays of cigars and decanters of brandy and whisky were brought around. General Pollock commandeered a three hundred-year-old Armagnac, which he swore to share solely with his "guest of honour, Captain Sparrowhawk". Such reverential treatment was more than Sparrowhawk could have hoped for. As the general insisted on filling his glass again and again with the vintage liquor, he became overly self-conscious about it.

"My lord, please … I am not worthy of this attention."

"Humility is a virtue, Sparrowhawk," Pollock rumbled, blowing out plumes of fragrant cigar smoke. "That is an old saying, which doubtless you've heard?"

"Of course."

"Another old saying is 'never hide one's light beneath a bushel'. You've heard that?"

"Yes."

"Excellent. It would ill become me to enlist an after-dinner speaker who had nothing to say for himself."

"After-dinner speaker?" Sparrowhawk was aware that he'd suddenly gone pale.

Pollock pealed with laughter, and again filled his guest's glass almost to its brim. "Don't look so worried, old chap. If necessary, I'll prompt you."

"My lord, I haven't … I haven't prepared …"

"Your service record is your preparation. None in here can match it, I'll wager." At which point Pollock stood up and, taking a spoon, rapped hard on the table. The music ceased and the room came quickly to order.

"Gentlemen, pray silence for our official guest of honour – formerly of the 16th Light Dragoons, in whose service he was mentioned in despatches three times, and on the last occasion received a brevet promotion. May I present Captain John William Sparrowhawk."

Loud, drunken applause greeted this, but Sparrowhawk's legs were trembling. Every eye in the room was suddenly fixed on him. He made to stand – only for the general to plant a massive hand on his shoulder and keep him in his seat.

"No need to stand on ceremony, captain. We're all friends and equals in this fraternity."

There were mumbles of "yes", "absolutely," "by Jove".

Pollock added: "Regale us, if you would, with the story of your heroism in Afghanistan."

Sparrowhawk smiled awkwardly. "These events are fully documented, my lord …"

"We'd like to hear them from your own lips."

"This is a Christmas banquet. It's not for me to put myself at the centre …"

"Every man has his time, captain. This is yours."

Sparrowhawk licked his lips. The room was so quiet that he could have heard a pin drop; the diners' attention was suddenly rapt. He hadn't been expecting this, but if it was to be compelled of him – he cleared his throat nervously, and commenced.

"Well … my first two mentions were for the actions at Kandahar in May '39 and Ghuznee in July that year. At Kandahar we provided a flanking guard for General Keane's advance, and moved onto high ground where the local khans were massing against us. We broke them in a single charge."

Cheers greeted this.

"At Ghuznee, we diverted from the besieging force to meet several thousand Ghilazi tribesmen, who had circled the city to attack Shah Shuja's brigade. I didn't do anything particularly courageous on either occasion, gentlemen, except that I was there both times and that I fought. Certainly, I was no braver than my men. At Ghuznee, we captured several antiquated cannon, which could have taken quite a toll of us when we stormed the city. We suffered relatively light casualties, for which I don't think we've ever thanked God enough given the savagery of the fighting."

Gradually, as he recollected events in that far off and mysterious land, his confidence to relate them grew. This wasn't something he enjoyed doing. In fact, he'd resisted it ever since returning to Britain. But if it served a purpose here, it was worth giving it everything he had.

"The Afghan tribesmen, for those of you who have not yet served over there, gentlemen, are formidable warriors, driven not just by an Islamic zeal but by a ferocious spirit of independence. Theirs was a military culture from ancient times. Alexander the Great made gains in Gandhara, which is part of eastern Afghanistan, but he lost numberless men in the process and none of his conquests lasted. The current Afghan warrior elite have changed little. They wage war either from foot or on horseback, and fight with spears, shields and scimitars, though they have also added the highly accurate 'jezail' musket to their arsenal, and have become deadly marksmen. Their main asset is their innate fearlessness, and the frenzy with which they fight."

"They're a brutal bunch, to be sure," Pollock interrupted, "and complete animals with their captives."

"That's always been a frightening aspect of war on the Sub-Continent, my lord," Sparrowhawk said.

"Tell us about Kabul, where you were breveted."

Again, Sparrowhawk cleared his throat. His audience seemed fascinated. Many of them looked too young to have experienced any combat for themselves.

"The situation that you refer to was really quite horrendous, my lord. After Kandahar and Ghuznee, we took possession of Kabul, and formed a regular garrison. When Dost Mohammed surrendered – he was the mogul who had been on the throne of Kabul prior to our arrival – it seemed that Afghanistan was pacified. An entire brigade was withdrawn, and civilians were soon arriving. It became like a small outpost of India. There were fetes and tea parties. Sir William Macnaghten, the Viceroy's envoy, even had a racecoure built. Some of the city's damaged fortifications were removed and never replaced. But the Afghan tribes hadn't gone away. They filled the mountains surrounding us, and there were incidents as far south as the Helmond River, with supply caravans being attacked along the Khyber. I began to worry that we were understrength and a long way from help should there be a major uprising. The appointment of General Elphinstone, with all respect to his rank, my lord …"

Pollock nodded as if this was no concern to him.

Sparrowhawk continued: "The appointment of General Elphinstone was the final nail in our coffin. He'd been a fine leader of men in his day – many a trooper in the Duke of Wellington's army would swear by his abilities – but he was elderly by this time and sick. He ignored reports from our scouts that the Ghilazi were gathering in strength. As part of the ongoing reduction, he ordered Brigadier Sale to take his companies south to Peshawar. The brigadier duly set off, but, as I understand it, he only made it as far as Jellalabad."

"I hear Sale then ignored orders from Elphinstone to return to Kabul?" Pollock said.

Sparrowhawk shrugged. "I doubt he had any choice, my lord. He'd been attacked all the way and, by the time he reached Jellababad, he had less than half the force he'd set out with. Back at Kabul, what remained of us was now completely cut off and the city encircled. There were even Afghan agents on the inside, and they caused constant trouble. Colonel Burnes, one of our more effective political officers, was murdered by an assassin. Macnaghten himself was killed attempting to parley with some Afghan emirs, who he fancied he could bribe to change sides and join us."

Sparrowhawk briefly paused. The memories were coming thick and fast – all stained with blood and powder, and enshrouded by the terrible atmosphere of doom that had soon come to pervade that ancient and embattled city.

"A siege had begun, though initially we hardly saw the enemy. There were no frontal attacks, which we could have repulsed effectively. Instead, they used the cover of the mountainsides, day and night firing on us from the high ground. I led a couple of sorties, but we only partially cleared them – and they always returned afterwards."

"When did Elphinstone opt to leave the city and retreat?" Pollock asked.

"The following January." Sparrowhawk shook his head, as appalled by such folly now as he had been at the time. "The worst possible month to be caught in the Afghan wilderness. He spoke to the Ghilazi and negotiated a safe passage to the Indian border, but only on the condition that we left most of our artillery behind."

"The damn, bloody fool!"

"Such a decision only added to our problems, my lord. It was a mere ninety miles to Jellalabad, but in my opinion we had a number of fatal weaknesses before we even set out. To start with, we were overburdened with civilians – almost twelve thousand."

There were groans from the assembled officers.

"We were also overburdened with infantry," Sparrowhawk

said. "I don't mean to decry the foot-sloggers, my lord, but in the vast, rocky desolation that is Afghanistan we should have been more mobile than we were. We had just over four thousand infantry, but the only mounted forces to hand were the Bengal Light Cavalry and our own 16th Light Dragoons, of which we had two squadrons serving under Major Cranbourne. Captain Prendergast was in charge of the lancers, while I had the hussars. That gave us a total of about nine hundred horse. Not nearly enough, gentlemen, as I'm sure you'll realise. We were also hindered by the presence of so many Indian troops. Don't get me wrong, sepoy companies have been among the most competent and reliable that I've ever served with. But at Kabul they were composed of Bengali foot, which are mainly Hindu. They were more frightened by Afghanistan than most because they deemed it to be outside of Hindustan. They were also affected by the cold. Much more than we northern Europeans were, though we were badly affected enough. The Afghan winter, gentlemen, makes this cold snap we're having in London feel like a mellow day in spring."

"That is definitely so," Pollock grunted.

"It's also worth noting," Sparrowhawk said, "that many of the Indians had their families with them. Some of the Essex and the Royal Anglians, who comprised the rest of the infantry, did as well. But the Indian troops particularly dreaded their wives and children falling into the hands of the Afghans. They assumed that British non-combatants would fare better – this was an incorrect assumption as it transpired, but nevertheless they believed it and were constantly in the extreme of fear. One thing we definitely could have used at such a time was a battalion of Ghurka Rifles – we'd had several with us until about a year earlier, but they'd all been withdrawn as part of General Elphinstone's reduction."

There were more groans.

"Despite the safe passage General Elphinstone had supposedly negotiated, we were assailed almost as soon as we left the Kabul redoubt."

Again, Sparrowhawk had to pause to conceal a tremor in his voice. It was astonishing, but this was the first time he'd felt strong emotion about what had happened. While in hospital in Peshawar, an army physician had told him that at some point he would let it all out – he would have to. No man could experience such a thing and shrug it off like a bad dream. Hopefully this banquet would not be that occasion, but he still had to steady himself before continuing.

"The Afghans were everywhere as soon as we were outside, pouring down from the mountains in their thousands. At first it was simple intimidation – wailing, shouting, shooting into the air. We marched in good order, but they were on all sides of us, and there were vastly more of them than we'd expected. The hillsides literally swarmed with them – horsemen, infantry. The dust they kicked up blotted out what little sun there was. I estimated they were fifty thousand strong."

He halted to dab his brow with a napkin. General Pollock offered him a brandy, and he took it gratefully.

"Before that first evening they were openly attacking us, both from close quarter and from a distance. We cavalry performed a circling rearguard, riding up and down the rear flanks of the column. This drew the sniper fire away from the civilians and onto us, and allowed us to meet head-on any groups of horsemen that approached. We engaged them frequently. There was much hand-to-hand stuff, but our numbers were soon depleted. Major Cranbourne was killed on the first morning, Captain Prendergast on the next. That put me in full command of the Dragoons, not that we had too many left by the end of that second day – I seem to recall it was something like three hundred."

The groans from the dining tables took on a note of disbelief.

"The nights were probably the worst. It was the bitterest weather imaginable, and there was never any shelter. We had snow, hail, blasting, icy wind. All we could do was huddle together in square, the civilians in the middle. The Afghans never stopped attacking. There were several full engagements in complete darkness. By the third day, we had a frightful bag of wounded, which slowed us down even more. Their horsemen now sallied into us at will. Every one of our soldiers, British and Indian, fought magnificently, but we were too few. Entire sections of the column were by this time undefended. The Afghans also applied mental pressure. If they could, they snatched stragglers and outriders alive rather than killed them. We then had to endure horrific screams as these poor devils were tortured. Sometimes we saw it. They were on ridges, impaled on stakes or hanging upside down over fires."

Pollock interrupted, in a voice so bass that it seemed to come from the pit of his belly. "The Afghans later argued that they were resisting oppression. They claimed that they had been invaded and were doing the only thing they could to preserve their country. They made this claim, gentlemen, shortly before my Army of Retribution put half their nation to the sword."

Roars of delight followed this. Spoons were thumped on tables in an outburst of spontaneous delight that Sparrowhawk felt he could not contribute to. When the noise had lessened, he continued his narrative.

"We lost many more while traversing the Khoord Cabul Pass. When they tried to follow us through, it enabled us to charge back at them on a narrow front. We slew hundreds in the process, and bought time for the rest of the column, but the gorge was five miles in length, and when we ourselves retreated, they were able to fire on us from above for the whole of that distance. On the sixth day of the march, General Elphinstone and Brigadier Shelton were both captured. We'd lost so many other senior ranks by then that our chain of command was shattered. Later that evening, with wind and snow swirling around us, we reached a place called Jugdulluk. Again the road was narrow, and the Ghizalzi had barricaded it against us with fences woven from thorns. We had some horse artillery remaining, and managed to blow holes in these bulwarks."

"And you, Captain Sparrowhawk, led the charge that broke

through, did you not?" Pollock said. "For which Medical Officer Bryden later said you should be breveted."

Sparrowhawk hung his head, unable to meet the admiring stares.

"I fear it was a futile effort, my lord. Thousands of them waited on the other side. We cleared some headway for what remained of the column, and then wheeled around to try and protect its rear. But night was falling by this time, and there was a sense of unmanageable panic. I opted to try to hold that position at the rear, but then my horse was killed beneath me. They'd brought up some of the smaller pieces of artillery that they'd already taken from us, three mountain guns, and were training them on us from high ground. As you can imagine, this was a catastrophic development."

Again, his voice almost broke, but he was determined to struggle on.

"Most of the lads were unhorsed by those first few salvos. The rest dismounted so that we could fight side-by-side with them. The Afghans came at us in overwhelming numbers. We responded with volley fire, dropping rank after rank, but there were always more. Soon they were among us and it was toe-to-toe. We fought them long into the night, but eventually we were annihilated. As … as was the rest of the column a few miles further along the road. It disintegrated in the impossible conditions. Those remaining women and children were cut down. The following morning, a company of infantry made a final stand on a hill called Gandamak. They died to the last man."

A deafening silence followed this, lasting nearly a minute.

"I was one of a handful of survivors," Sparrowhawk eventually said. "The only one from the Dragoons. I'd been wounded twice by the time we reached Jugdulluk. I was wounded again in that final fight. I passed out from blood loss, but survived the night lying among the dead. In the morning, the Afghans ignored us further to converge on Gandamak. I was able to slip away on a lamed horse. I arrived at Jellalabad several days

84

later, having picked my way through the bleakest mountain passes imaginable. Why anyone would even *want* to conquer Afghanistan, my lord, is still beyond me."

Pollock shrugged. "Whatever the East India Company sets its sights on, Sparrowhawk. You know that."

Sparrowhawk nodded.

"You're aware of course that we later we took a grandiose revenge?" Pollock said.

"I am, my lord."

"My Army of Retribution fought its way up the Khyber Pass in a single day," Pollock said, to renewed loud cheering. "At Huft Kotal I met Akhbar Khan in pitched battle and slew fifteen thousand of his men, sending the cowardly dog fleeing from the field with bullets whistling around his ears. On the march to Kabul, we saw the wreckage of Elphinstone's retreat. Entire companies reduced to bleached bones. The skeletons of British and Indian families lying huddled together, embracing each other even in death. It hardened my lads' resolve. We destroyed every village we came to, massacring its occupants. In Kabul itself, we burned the mosque and the bazaar. My agents told me the Kohistannee tribe had been heavily involved in the atrocities, so I singled them out for special treatment. We bombarded their capital of Charikar to rubble, and slaughtered its entire population. Afterwards, we destroyed their crops and sewed the ground with salt, condemning the remainder to starvation in a wasteland of their own making."

Such rapturous applause greeted this that the room seemed ready to explode. Officers jumped from their chairs and rushed forwards to embrace the two "heroes of Kabul", as they proclaimed them. Amid a tumult of noise and backslapping, Sparrowhawk's arm was pumped by one young chap after another.

"Well done!" they bellowed into his ear. "Well done, by God!" For General Pollock it was more a case of: "You showed those murdering heathens, sir! By jingo, they felt British steel when you

85

arrived! You're quite the fellow!"

To Sparrowhawk it all seemed painfully misplaced, but as he had seemingly been required to relate these events, he now realised that it was also required of him to accept deification because of them. He thus kept his objections to himself. Besides, he was soon distracted by the sight of a liveried footman arriving alongside General Pollock with his cocked hat and riding cloak.

"Gentlemen, please!" Pollock boomed. "I regret to say that I must take my leave. This has been a grand occasion, but alas I have one more engagement before the night is done. This room, however, is yours until first light. There is more food, more wine, more spirits – pray, help yourselves. Eat and drink as much as you wish, and then eat and drink some more in honour of the season."

There were gales of raucous laughter.

"My lord, if I might have a word in private?" Sprarrowhawk said, attempting to take his host to one side.

Pollock raised a bushy eyebrow. This close, he looked more like a lion than ever. His golden eyes were saucer shaped, his very breath seemed to rumble as it slipped in and out of his capacious chest. It reeked of brandy and cigar smoke, but there was something below this that was vaguely unpleasant – blood maybe?

"As I say, captain, I do have a second engagement."

"I understand, my lord, but it would be a great help if you could spare me one minute." Sparrowhawk flicked ash from his cheroot. "I'm overwhelmed by your kind words this evening, but times have been hard for me – I could use some advice."

"In that case, captain …" The general positioned his hat on his head, and threw his cloak over his shoulders, fastening it across his chest with a brass chain. He nodded towards the double-doors connecting with the kitchen. "This way!"

"After you, sir."

Pollock nodded and went first. As he reached the kitchen doors, Sparrowhawk pushed him from behind, putting all his weight into it. The general tottered forwards, slamming into the doors. They swung open and he staggered through them. Sparrowhawk followed, jamming his cheroot between his teeth.

On the other side, there was no scene of organised chaos: no cooks, washerwomen or livery-clad waiters rushed back and forth. No worktops were covered with cutlery or used crockery. In fact there were no worktops at all. It was a dismal brick chamber, paved with wet stone and frigid with cold. The only light was provided by frosty moonbeams penetrating the grimy glass panels on a sliding wooden door at its far end. General Pollock staggered forwards several yards. But then regained his balance, and swung around, a bulky silhouette. When he growled this time, it was the growl of a genuine lion: rolling and thunderous.

"You are indeed quite the fellow, my lord," Sparrowhawk said, "to be in two places at once."

The silhouetted figure merely growled again. Its hat had already come off. Now it discarded its cloak, and slowly, pointedly drew off its gloves. Below them, even in the dimness, Sparrowhawk saw an immense pair of paw-like hands: thick curly fur covered the backs of them – no doubt it would be tawny in colour; curved nails that were more like claws adorned the end of each finger.

"You think I'd be so easily fooled?" Sparrowhawk said. "You think I'd accept your bogus invitation at face-value? You think I wouldn't check and very quickly discover that General Pollock is in fact still in India with his regiments? You think I'd be so flattered by your interest in me that I'd spend the whole night wallowing in food, drink and adulation when I'm supposed to be on duty? You think I'd be so seduced by these gifts that I'd let you just walk out of here and keep your second and more important engagement – at 48, Doughty Street?"

"There are two types of people in this world, Captain Sparrowhawk," the lion-thing rumbled, taking the collar of its tunic and rending it open. "Those who pick the battlefield, and those who are lured to it. Aren't you tired yet of being among the latter?" With a single jerk, it tore its tunic off like tissue paper.

"Sometimes it pays to fight away from home," Sparrowhawk replied. "The secret of any battlefield is making the best of it."

"When they first summoned me, they told me you'd be a worthy opponent."

"Worthy of who – you?" Sparrowhawk laughed. "You, who must first weaken his enemy with drink before you try to skulk away!"

"Don't overestimate yourself, captain. Weakness and drink are a human trait, particularly at this time of year. You may have uncommmon strengths, but you too have drunk deep from the well this night."

"And maybe not." From behind his back, Sparrowhawk produced a lidded tankard sloshing with liquid. "An old soldier's canteen, in case you can't recognise it – which I strongly suspect, as I doubt you've ever been near a real battle. There's more than enough room in this to contain the sixteen brandies you attempted to ply me with during dinner."

With another low growl – this one mewling and prolonged – the lion-thing tore off its dress shirt. The naked torso beneath was massive of shoulder and chest, padded all over with muscle, rich with thick, tawny fur. The monster now hunched low, the entire room reverberating to its growls. Fleetingly Sparrowhawk saw its eyes again: pits of molten gold. With an ear-splitting roar, it charged, still on two legs but in a stooped, gambolling run, swerving in and out of the moonlight to mask its aproach.

Sparrowhawk knew that it would leap on him and tear him apart, snap his limbs, flay the flesh from his ribs, clamp his skull with its colossal jaws, its ivory teeth sinking like bayonets through skin and bone. But he held his ground, as he always had, and at the last second took a huge draught from the canteen, flicked his cheroot, and, placing its lighted end in the firing line, blew out a billowing cloud of fire, which *whooshed* into the lion-thing, engulfing its entire head and upper body.

Its guttural roar became a shrill howl as it flinched away, its features visibly seared, its shaggy mane alight. It swiped at him with its paw, but he stepped aside and poured more brandy down its back. Liquid flame followed.

"Sorry general!" he shouted. "A rather nasty party-trick I learned during another misspent evening in the officers' mess!"

The thing spun around to strike at him again, only for him to douse its barrel chest, the fire now descending towards its crotch. When he soaked its trousers, they too caught. The thing was now ablaze from head to foot. It caromed from wall to wall, a living torch, the air around it rank with smoke and the stench of charring flesh. Sparrowhawk stepped after it, throwing brandy until the canteen was empty.

Shrieking like a castrato, it stumbled and fell across the room, at last locating its cloak, which it wrapped around itself. As the flames died, the smoke and the stench thickened. The hybrid horror had finally extinguished itself, but its struggles were suddenly feeble. It lay on the flagstones shuddering, mewling again – like a sickly cat.

Sparrowhawk threw the canteen away, drew his sabre and dropped to his knees. When he ripped aside the smouldering cloth, a burned travesty of a face peered up at him. It was still half way between lion and man, but its mane and its pelt had been singed to blackened stubble. Its flesh was slick with melted fat. The eyes it regarded him with were tarnished jewels, buried in blistered purulence.

"There are two types of people in this, my friend," Sparrowhawk said, raising his sabre. "Those who wield the steel, and those who take it. You, it may surprise you to learn, are among the latter."

"But I'm not alone," the thing rasped, smoke issuing from its shrivelled lips. "How many … how many have taken steel in your place, Captain Sparrowhawk? How many more have still to take it?"

A chill ran up Sparrowhawk's spine as the wounded monstrosity began to laugh – to actually laugh, in fact to laugh at

89

him. At first it was a choked snicker, but it grew rapidly in strength. Soon the beast was roaring in scornful and triumphant mirth. With a strangled cry, Sparrowhawk slashed down, severing its head with a single blow.

Tempted though he was, to take the grisly trophy by what remained of its mane, and carry it away with him, he was now too sickened by stink and filth. He toppled back to his feet and pushed through the doors to the eating hall. He wasn't sure what he expected to find in there, but he was stumped by the sight that met him. The ornate Christmas chamber had vanished – instead it was a bare brick hangar. Where the jolly fire had crackled in the hearth now there were only dull, red flames, the vile smoke of which hung below the ceilng in a dirty blanket. Neither food nor drink was present, but all the tables and chairs remained – though this time they contained different occupants.

"Sergeant Cobley?" Sparrowhawk stuttered. "Lieutenant Cooper …"

The 16th Light Dragoons had arrived. Their dark blue jackets decorated with silver braid and scarlet facings bore testimony to this, though to a layman such garb would be unrecognisble so slashed and hacked was it, so charred and torn and coated with blood and ordure. The men wearing it were in no better condition. Though each was seated in a dining place, he either slumped forwards on the table or hung from his chair. Sergeant Cobley's legs ended at the ragged stumps of his knees. There was an entry hole in Lieutenant Cooper's forehead and an exit wound at the rear, where half his skull had been blown away. Captain Prendergast's head was hinged backwards, revealing a throat slit to the spinal cord. Corporal Crooks was transfixed to his chair by a spear. Trooper Benbridge had been ripped apart from neck to crotch, and his innards scattered. Major Cranbourne occupied the seat that General Pollock had used; his jaw was a mass of shattered bone, a musket ball still visibly lodged in it.

From one end of the room to the next, the blasted, shredded relics of Sparrowhawk's command were gathered like beggars at a banquet of the damned. Only one seat was empty – the one he himself had occupied, but, even as he stared at it, a misty shape was swirling into being there from the vile ether of this smoke-filled charnel house. He had no desire to see who this would be, but already a terrible suspicion was forming in his tortured mind.

A shriek tore from Sparrowhawk's chest as he ran for the main doors.

Barging out into the frozen night, he found himself in a rubble-strewn courtyard; the pristine snow that filled it was disturbed only by his own tracks and those of Peppercorn, who stood there untethered, waiting and tossing her head. Sparrowhawk leapt into the saddle. He took one look at the building where he had just dined – though dined on what, for he no longer felt replete but hollow and hungry, as though he'd been gnawing on roots and berries? – and saw not an officer's mess nor a club of any sort, but a derelict outbuilding attached to yet another of the East India Company endless, dreary warehouses.

He wheeled the horse around and put his heels to its flanks. They galloped pell-mell through the glistening white streets. He should have refuted the adulation from the outset, of course. Even though his behaviour had been part of a ruse, he should have told them forcefully that there'd been nothing romantic about the 16th Light Dragoons' final action at Jugdulluk, little that was heroic in such a gory calamity.

His men were in a pitiful state that last evening: famished, frostbitten, filthy, their uniforms in rags, their limbs and bodies swathed with gangrenous bandages. They'd fought bravely, there was no question. So long as they delayed the Afghans from pursuing the rest of the column, they knew it was a stand worth making. The sights from the previous couple of nights had bolstered their resolve: the civilian contingent at its wits' end; children crying with cold and hunger, the wives crying with fear, the English women offering their spare clothes to the Indian women, hoping to fool the Afghans, but knowing in their hearts that it would be futile for all of them.

Cheers and guffaws and cries of "hear hear" and "by jingo" were one thing, But the *real* memories of that last desperate stand had never stopped haunting Sparrowhawk.

Tribesmen were surging on all sides, their powerful jezails pouring non-stop fire into the close-packed British ranks. In return, the cavalry troopers' carbines were less effective, lacking the range of an infantryman's rifle or even the old 'Brown Bess' musket. Sparrowhawk had always preferred his Greener. It was easy to wield from the saddle, and at close quarter could be devastating – as he proved when the Afghans finally charged in. Standing astride the mangled hulk of Cleo, his slain mount, he discharged barrel after barrel at them, mowing down three or four of them at a time, blowing multiple holes in their flesh. But he'd been hurt before this final confrontation had even started. In the Khoord Cabul Pass, a sniper had shot off his shako, the musket ball glancing from the top of his skull, leaving a shallow but gruesome wound, which bled continuously and had proved impossible to dress. As such, his face and tunic had been drenched with blood for most of the march from that point on. At the charge through the thorn fence, a scimitar had bitten into his right thigh, partly severing the nerves. As such, when the fight at Jugdulluk became hand-to-hand, Sparrowhawk's strength quickly ebbed.

When his Greener was knocked from his grasp, he drew his sabre and cut his way among them. He hacked an Afghan's legs away. He shore another's arm at the elbow. He rammed his sword through a screaming mouth, only for the blade to snap as he tried to yank it free – and now he was dizzy with effort. Shadows leapt all around him. There was a clangour of blade on blade, a chorus of shrieks and screams, of fire-filled detonations as guns were discharged from pointblank range. Musket balls whistled, steel *chunked* as it sheared flesh and clove bone. The mingled stench of bowels and gore and vomit was almost suffocating.

Sparrowhawk retrieved his Greener from a rocky ground

greased with blood and human entrails. A figure lunged at him – he fired. In the blinding flash, a Ghizali was hurled backwards, his face torn from the fragmented skull beneath. Sparrowhawk had no time to reload before he was struck in the back – the butt of a jezail slamming between his shoulders. He gagged at the pain, but turned and again fired, discharging his last barrel into two of them at once – both ripped asunder at the midriff, their blood and meat showering him with hot, smoky rain. He choked and wretched, but then gasped as a poniard was thrust into his right side, slicing two of his ribs like sticks of celery.

In the pitch darkness he could only smell and feel the sweat-soaked enemy who now grappled with him, but that was sufficient to stab him with the broken sabre, again and again until his last ounce of strength gave. When Sparrowhawk finally sagged to the ground, breath and blood venting from his body at a hideous rate, his final opponent slid down on top of him, masking him for the dawn when the triumphant Afghans would rampage across the field like hyenas, pillaging and savaging the bodies of the slain before heading off to Gandamak to complete the annihilation of the hated invaders.

"Daniel!" he shouted, jumping from Peppercorn's back.

Doughty Street was under a deeper chill than he'd ever known in England, the temperatures having plunged to an incalculable low. The snow itself had frozen so hard that the horse's hooves barely made an impression on it.

Trooper Willoughby was where Sparrowhawk had left him, standing behind the rhododendrons. His face was fixed in a smile, possibly in gratitude that he'd been made to feel useful again – but it was also covered in frost. The shotgun was concealed inside his greatcoat, as Sparrowhawk had instructed. Willoughby's hands were in there too, tucked away in a last futile attempt to keep warm.

Sparrowhawk's tears froze as quickly as they fell, as he dragged the blue and rigid form across the park and laid it in a snowy grave some distance from Doughty Street, where it might at length be discovered and written off as a vagrant who hadn't found shelter. Dawn was now breaking, so Sparrowhawk collected his shotgun and shells, and rode doggedly back to Camden Town.

XI

On returning to Camden Town, Sparrowhawk first wrote a long letter, and posted it to 13, Rislington Row, Eastcheap, before climbing into bed and sleeping dreamlessly until evening came. By this time a fog had descended on central London so dense that visibility was nonexistent. There'd still been no thaw. When he returned to Doughty Street, the snow and ice crunched underfoot, but now with a hollow echo, the fog creating an eerie 'indoor' atmosphere.

That next night was the loneliest he'd thus far spent, but he bore through it with the knowledge that it would be his last. Seeing no-one at all, not even a nightwatchman or a strolling peeler, made him feel isolated and vulnerable. Instead of cloaking him, he wondered if the fog was cloaking others. Once he thought he heard distant squawking laughter, like a demented puppet. Another time, there was the faint sound of a bugle playing *The Last Post*. He didn't rise to either of these baits, but continued to inspect the front and rear of the premises, keeping constantly on the move so that he could retain a modicum of warmth – something that poor Dan Willoughby had been unable to do. At last the morning came and, as far as Sparrowhawk was concerned, the job was done. Instead of returning to Camden Town and sleeping, he took Peppercorn back to the stable, and headed south on foot, finally opting to take his breakast – which would be exclusively of the liquid variety – at *The Moon O'er The Mire* on Jacob's Island.

At this early hour of the day, only a handful of ruffians and painted doxies were present. Some were asleep in corners. Others were bleary eyed and brutally hungover. The landlord and his skivies were doing what they could to clean the place up, replacing the coals in the hearth, laying fresh straw, bringing in new barrels from the storehouse at the rear. Sparrowhawk, still in his working garb and looking haggard and unshaven from his long watch, fitted in comfortably. No questions were asked when

95

he ordered a mug of rum and a flagon of beer, and retired to the corner where he'd first located Willoughby.

Only a few minutes passed, before someone else sat at his table. It was one of the women. She wore a pretty bonnet with dyed-pink ostrich plumes, but this only served to accentuate the drabness of the rest of her attire. Her dress was also pink, and formerly had been a mass of frills and lace, but now was faded and ragged, revealing the stained chemise beneath. Her bodice had been patched several times, but was still missing buttons. Her face, though dabbled with blusher and rouge, was extraordinarily pretty – which seemed strange given the life these impoverished creatures lived. But then Sparrowhawk smelled rose and jasmine, and he understood.

"I almost didn't recognise you," he said.

Miss Evangeline placed his letter on the table. "So you've resigned again?"

He drank more beer. "I have."

"You realise what this means?"

"I'm quite prepared for it. If you've been able to find me already, I expect the bailiffs will have no trouble arresting me by this afternoon."

"On what grounds can the bailiffs arrest you? Your debt has been paid."

"You said you'd bill my bail back to the court."

"A little white lie. As I told you when we first met, we didn't make you a loan. You owe us nothing."

Sparrowhawk was puzzled. "You're not concerned that your man will be unprotected for this final week?"

"Not at all. Because he won't be. I have no intention of allowing you to resign."

He snorted with laughter. "You talk as if you think you can force me. Nothing you can do to me could be worse than what I've endured these last two days."

"And what is that?"

"What do you think? Yet another man died when it should

96

have been me."

He took a long, hard pull on his flagon, draining it completely. Banging it down, he shouted for the landlord to send him another. Miss Evangeline watched in silence as the second drink was served and the requisite coppers were thrown into the wench's apron.

"Why exactly did you go to the Officers' Club?" Miss Evangeline asked.

"Does it matter? The fact is I was there when I should have been somewhere else."

"It matters a great deal. Did you go there because you wanted to drink brandy, smoke cigars and partake in the glorification of conquest?"

"I went because I hoped to meet this nebulous, nameless menace in person. Again, I was trying to avoid fighting him on home ground."

"So, in that respect would you not say that your motives were actually for the best?"

He took another long drink. "Easy for the likes of us to say. We're still alive."

"Captain, why did you survive the battle of Jugdulluk when all the rest of your men died? Did you run away?"

He stiffened. "You know I didn't."

"So?"

"It was luck."

"Only luck? But you accepted your hero's laurels afterwards."

"I didn't want to refuse them." He fidgeted. "But I never felt good about it."

"That's understandable. Sole survivors often feel that way. But tell me this, captain: what would be the best thing – for *most* to die, or *all* to die?"

"Forgive me, Miss Evangeline, I find it difficult to be so coldly logical when we're talking about the lives of my friends. Besides, there was never any logic to the war in Afghanistan. Either its reasons or its conduct. Have you ever heard the cries of women and children when they're being cruelly slaughtered?"

"Yes, I have."

That surprised him, though he supposed by now that it shouldn't do.

"In which case, you'll know that no amount of horror in the world can match it," he said. "The Army of Retribution wreaked similar atrocities to those we suffered. And then they left – just like that, *left!* I ask you, if we saw so little value in capturing and holding Afghanistan, why did we go there in the first place?"

"You know the answer to that, Captain Sparrowhawk. The Tsar was expanding into Asia. Afghanistan might have been the key to a Russian invasion of India."

He shook his head. "This game of chess won't go on forever. Some day soon we'll be fighting the Russians themselves, and then there'll be unparalleled bloodshed. Do you ever wonder, Miss Evangeline, if any of our colonies, or even all of them together, are worth the lives of so many?"

She looked shocked. "You don't believe in the British Empire, captain?"

"Once… maybe." He took another long drink, again draining his flagon. "When I held it to be a force for good, a civilising influence. But my father was right. It's a vast arrogance to assume that people will accept servitude in their own land. In fact it's worse than that, it's rank foolishness."

"And how is this realisation relevant to the incident of two nights ago?"

"If you must know …" He signalled for a third flagon. "In Afghanistan I was serving a master whose aims are, at the very best, doubtful. Two nights ago I was serving a master whose aims are completely unknown to me."

"So it's a question of morality?"

"Let me put it this way … I don't think that working for you is improving me as a person."

"And is *that?*" she asked, as his third flagon of beer was delivered.

"This isn't hurting anyone."

"In our service, Captain Sparrowhawk, you've so far confronted two strange and unpleasant beings. Do you deny that they were evil?"

"The main evil they invoked was in me."

"And they rejoiced in it. Did it not give you pleasure to vanquish them?"

He considered this, before saying: "It was too costly. My resignation stands. I hope you can find someone else for this last week."

She sighed. "I shall certainly try."

The tavern door swung open to admit an old blind man and his dog. There was a bitter blast from the alley outside. The fog, which was so filled with suspended ice crystals that it was almost pearlescent, flowed in.

"Gad!" Sparrowhawk said. "I know it's the deep of winter, but this degree of cold is unnatural for London."

"Of course it is," Miss Evangeline agreed. "But it will be a two-edged sword."

"I don't understand."

"One man's misery is another man's inspiration." She stood up and offered her arm. "Come, walk with me."

"Walk with you?"

"You should be hardened to the cold by now."

"I'm not frightened of the cold, miss. I just don't see what purpose walking in it will serve."

"It will please me. Come … I walked with you, did I not?"

Reluctantly, he helped her with her shawl, put on his hat, and allowed her to lead him outside. White, frozen vapour filled the warren of passages and backstreets. Yet only five minutes' walk from *The Moon O'er The Mire,* they came to a place where a number of old men, old women and young children, little more than huddled bundles of rags, moved from one section of street to the next, sifting through the straw and the trampled, filthy snow.

"These people are 'pure-finders'," Miss Evangeline said.

"I know," he replied.

"They are hoping to find fresh, moist dog turds, which they can mix with dry mortar and sell in bulk to the tanneries."

"I know."

She led him down another passage, and they came to a wharf overlooking the Thames, large portions of which had actually frozen over – apparently for the first time in a hundred years. Despite this, and the even thicker veils of fog which seemed to pulse along the river as they watched, small, skeletal figures, many barefoot, were visibly prowling the exposed sewerage and mud-banks, eagerly pouncing on any treasure they found – be it a bone, a nail, a piece of rope, an unbroken bottle – and stuffing it into a sack.

"These people survive by selling riverside detritus," Miss Evangeline said, to which Sparrowhawk again wearily replied that he was already aware of it.

On a Bermondsey street corner, they encountered a group of crossing-sweepers, who were doing better than normal at this time of year, as gentlefolk were more likely to tip them for removing snow and ice from the pavements than dust. In Rotherhithe, the fog broke briefly to show a donkey drawing a cart, on which were perched a chimney sweep and three young children, all of them black from head to foot with tar and soot. The blankets that wrapped the youngsters, and the disused newspapers with which they'd bound their feet, were equally dirty. Miss Evangeline pointed out that even though it was now illegal for sweeps to use 'climbing boys', it was still a regular occurrence as the penalties were pitifully small – at which point Sparrowhawk's patience gave out.

"What are you trying to prove?" he snapped. "That there's abject squalour in the bowels of the Empire? I already know that. You think I didn't see it for myself in the Fleet? You think my father didn't hammer it into me?"

"Eliciting your sympathy for the underclass, Captain Sparrowhawk, would be a complete waste of time," she replied.

"In your reduced circumstances, you wouldn't be in a position to help them even if you were minded to. What I'm showing you here is… industriousness."

"Industriousness?" he said, stunned. "Tortured wretches eking out a living in the filthiest conditions imaginable?"

"It's tragic, I grant you. But, in a strange and convoluted way, is it not impressive? That at least some are prepared to perform these tasteless but essential tasks?"

"Society won't collapse if children are taken out of chimneys or the mudlarks stop picking scrap off the riverbanks."

"*Their* society might." Miss Evangeline seemed quite serious. "These are their allotted tasks, Captain Sparrowhawk, and they perform them in most cases without complaint, unperturbed by the hideousness of the experience." She regarded him carefully, and he knew what was coming next. "You have a task too, captain. Are you prepared to show similar fortitude – or will you choose to turn your back, again?"

He rubbed at his brow. The brief effects of the alcohol were already wearing off. His head ached slightly. "You're saying I *must* complete the vigil?"

"If not for the good of all, for the good of yourelf."

"Myself, eh? Well that's just it. This sentry duty you've posted me on seems to be taking a very personal turn."

"And it will get worse." She took his arm and walked on. "The third and final visitant to Doughty Street will be the most terrible of all, and will test you beyond anything you've experienced in your life to this point. That said, we feel that after your previous encounters you are stoic enough to persevere."

"Who are you?" he asked. "Please, I need to know."

"I'm a servant, captain. Just as you are."

"Are you a ghost, maybe?"

It seemed like a bizarre question, but it was an easy thing to imagine in this world of swirling vapour, which though it as usual smelled of coke and sulphur, was still spectral white and searingly cold. All objects except those very close up were blotted out.

Torches and lanterns were vague red orbs passing back and forth. The rattles of cartwheels, the clatter of feet on crackling ice were dull, muffled thuds.

Miss Evangeline looked amused by the notion. "A ghost?"

"What else am I to think?" he said. "With your wisdom, your looks, your poise. Frankly, you're too perfect to be real. And I've had a bellyful of the unreal."

He made to move away, but she stopped him, turned his face to hers, and, standing up on tip toes, kissed him on the lips. Her mouth was warm, moist, sweet as rosewater. It lingered on his for several moments.

When they separated again, she asked: "Am I real enough for you now?"

He peered down at her. As he'd already noted, even made up as a drabtail, she was alluringly handsome.

"I may need more evidence," he said hoarsely.

"I warned you before … this path could end in tears."

"Every path I take ends in tears. I'm used to it."

"It could end in tears for me, as well. And I'm *not* used to it."

He leaned towards her. "I'm sorry, but victory requires sacrifice."

Their lips met again. His loins stirred as their tongues entwined. His muscles tightened as her hands crept around his back, the contours of her body fitting snugly against his. Suddenly, for the first time in months, Sparrowhawk felt strong again, healthy, vital – only for a loud, irritating knocking sound to distract them.

It came from a window in a wall close by. A red-faced man wearing lush side-whiskers and a pair of small, round spectacles was on the other side.

"You ragamuffin!" he shouted at Sparrowhawk. "These are respectable workshops! Take your round-the-corner-Sally somewhere else!"

Sparrowhawk stepped quickly backwards.

"My apologies," he said to Miss Evangeline. "This is not the way it should be done."

"It shouldn't be done at all," she replied under her breath, but she didn't object when he stopped a hackney and asked that they both be given a ride to Camden Town.

They travelled the whole distance in silence. When he tried to take her hand, she allowed him to, but she said nothing and gazed out of the window, looking vaguely distressed. This was not lost on him, even though in the space of two brief kisses his desire for her, latent since they'd first met, had become overwhelming. When they arrived, he climbed down into the courtyard first, but, when she tried to follow, he leaned on the door so that she couldn't open it.

"I've been grossly presumptuous," he said. "I'll have the driver take you on to Eastcheap. I'll even pay the extra fare."

"You've not been presumptuous," she replied, showing surprising strength to open the door against him and climb down.

"In which case I've bullied you into this … ?"

"Captain Sparrowhawk, I'm never bullied into anything."

When they entered his small suite of rooms, he said: "It isn't much. But of course you already know that, don't you?"

She said nothing; her eyes glistened as though wet with tears.

"For Heaven's sake, Miss Evangeline, let's call a halt to this! I'll walk you back to Eastcheap now, and I'll still watch Doughty Street until the vigil is served. I'll not have you prostitute yourself."

"I'll stay." She touched his cheek. "You need female companionship, as you've said. Of course you do. And if this will gird you for the fight …"

"I'd rather hoped that we'd *both* get something out of it."

"Never fear." Button by button, she unfastened her ragged dress. "We will."

XII

When he awoke early that evening, Miss Evangeline had left. This was as he'd expected, and didn't trouble him overly. Doubtless he would see her again soon. But he now felt he understood what she'd meant by 'girding him for the fight'. As darkness fell, he bought himself a hot pie before collecting Peppercorn and heading to Bloomsbury, but it wasn't the flavoursome pastry or rich meat contents that warmed him that night. An ardour burned in his breast the like of which he'd never known. He was almost giddy with it, a condition he knew he would have to shake off as the night wore on – not that he particularly wanted to.

The fog had lifted, and the sky was ablaze with stars. The snow lay deep and pristine. It was easy to be lulled by such seasonal scenery, but the horror and grief of the events two nights ago had not been expunged completely. Sparrowhawk knew that evil things lurked nearby; he knew that even now one of them was preparing to strike. And yet, his heart was thumping not with fear or trepidation, but with longing for that bewitching woman. The memory of their afternoon would stay with him for a considerable time: the red firelight dappling the walls and ceiling, rippling on Miss Evangeline's perfectly scultped form, on her supple limbs, on her honey-gold hair, which, once she'd untied it, had poured down her back in glimmering tresses.

It had all seemed so right. They'd brought each other effortlessly to fits of rapture as they'd woven their bodies in his warm, narrow bed. And this hadn't been some game she was playing with him, some pretence of passion; her cries and langorous moans would have been heard outside had there been anyone to hear. What was more, between these vigorous bouts, there'd been genuine tender moments. They'd dozed together and nuzzled each other. He'd kissed her sweetly, and she'd almost wept as she ran her fingertips and then her lips along the hard, jagged scars that criss-crossed his body.

"Could you ever feel the same way about me that I think I feel about you?" he'd asked her, as they'd lain in each other's arms, damp with perspiration.

"Captain Sparrowhawk …"

"Enough of this 'captain'. Call me John, please. That's my name."

"John … you barely know me. You can't have lost your heart so quickly?" She'd asked this anxiously, as though she was conflicted about the answer he might give.

"It's hardly been quick. Two weeks of the coldest nights London has ever seen, each one dragging like a lifetime. So could you…?"

"Possibly." She'd refused to look him in the eye. "I honestly don't know."

As he stood behind the snow-caked rhododendrons, he pondered this enigmatic answer. She hadn't been willing to commit herself to a relationship. On one hand that was disappointing; it meant she wasn't certain about him. But on the other it might be good; it might mean that he was winning her over slowly, extinguishing her reservations one by one, which would make for a more lasting alliance. Though why he sought an alliance he still wasn't entirely sure. It was true what she'd said, that he barely knew her. Any man would desire her; that was a given. But to suddenly want her to much? To suddenly *need* her?

Perhaps his current bleak condition, and her mysterious, captivating manner – one moment stiff and aloof, the next playful, teasing, and then the fulsome way she'd suddenly given herself to him – had proved an incendiary mix. Maybe it was no surprise that his emotions had been fired.

"This might be a happy Chistmas for me, after all," he'd told her. "I've never known one before. My mother died giving birth to me, so she had no influence on the celebration of the season. Father marked it but didn't believe, so there was no real purpose or soul to it. And after 1825, I barely noticed Christmas at all."

"This will be a Christmas like no other, John, I promise you," she'd said, kissing his cheek. "Sleep now. You may have another difficult night ahead."

But as it turned out, this was the least difficult night of them all. Sparrowhawk was too elated to feel bored or drowsy or even cold. He watched the house, and patrolled the neighbourhood, and saw and heard nothing suspcious. If he himself was being watched, he no longer cared. He was a man enflamed, and a man enflamed could meet any challenge without a qualm.

XIII

This depth of feeling grew as the night progressed, so much that, when he returned to Camden Town the following morning, he was disappointed not to find her waiting for him.

In fact it went further than mere disappointment. He was worried by it, even unnerved. He stood in his Spartan bedroom, staring at his bed, which, as always, he'd made up in regulation fashion, and it was easy to imagine that he hadn't shared an afternoon with anyone here, that in fact Miss Evangeline had never even been in the apartment. It wasn't just that there was no physical trace of her – there was no scent of rose and jasmine, no afterglow. The rooms seemed cold, dead.

So intense did this irrational concern become that Sparrowhawk didn't go straight to sleep, but went out again and visited the various taverns and eateries where she'd said he could contact her. She wasn't in any of them, which almost panicked him. It was only when he blundered across Tottenham Court Road, and was nearly run down by a coach and four which had trouble stopping on the ice, that reality intruded and he realised that he'd better get a grip on himself.

It was astonishing how quickly this attraction for Miss Evangeline had grown. He wondered if, for the first time in his life, he was actually in love. He'd always dismissed the notion of love as foolishness, something for moon-faced youngsters to indulge themselves with – but now he was less sure.

In an effort to reinstate his colder, more cynical self, he wandered the city for several hours, looking for distractions. Christmas week was approaching, of course, and London was dressing itself properly for the occasion. The markets and bazaars, particularly around Soho Square and the Pantheon, were decked with evergreens and crepe paper, and laden with wares of even more questionable quality than usual – from the feathers of rare birds to artificial flowers, from second-hand books to alabaster ornaments, from hand-me-down trinkets to hand-me-down clothes. On the great shopping boulevards like Oxford Street and Bond Street, a higher standard of commodity was on offer: the perfumeries boasting an array of exotic oils and creams; the tobacconists replacing their commonplace clay pipes with cigar cases, meerschaums and snuff boxes; the milliners, the lace sellers, the glovers, the hosiers, the drapers all displaying their most sumputous finery. William Hamley's toy shop, the famous Noah's Ark of High Holborn, was a particular wonder to behold, its candle-lit windows filled with ornate figurines formed from sugar and candy and wrapped with colourful foil, or made from wood and clockwork and painted in the Germanic fashion – all drawn from myth, magic and pantomime: soldiers, wizards, fairy queens, harlequins, ogres, witches. Numerous small children, buried in fur and velvet, their caps and bonnets pulled around their frost-nipped ears, their mittened hands clasped tightly by parent or governess, gazed pink-faced in wonder through the mullioned glass.

Next door to it, there was a jewellers, which Sparrowhawk found himself lured into. Here, he bought Miss Evangeline a gift: a small gold neck-chain with a jade pendant attached. It wasn't hugely expensive, but it was simple and pretty, and Miss Evangeline knew better than anyone the 'journeyman' wages he was earning. He had it Christmas-wrapped, but had to strongly fight the temptation to go to Eastcheap and hand it to her personally. Number 13, Rislington Row was an address she'd bade him attend only in cases of extreme emergency. To break a strict rule of his employment purely because he'd developed feelings for someone – an outcome that she'd cautioned him about repeatedly – would show a distinct lack of professionalism.

Instead, he posted the gift to her, and continued to stroll, determined to sober himself, which wasn't too difficult. To move between the thronging, glittering thoroughfares, one had to pass through more dingy alleys and narrow ways, filled with drunkards and ragged folk whose only interest at this time of year was to try to keep warm, and it reminded Sparrowhawk again that

Christmas was not a joyful time for everybody – though ironically it also reminded him of his walk with Miss Evangeline through Southwark, and his heart began to race again.

It was no matter, he tried to reassure himself. He needn't obsess over her. Everything was under control, and in due couse Miss Evangeline would reappear.

But she didn't.

And neither did the third visitant that she'd warned him about.

The temperature remained well below freezing for the rest of that week, particularly during the hours of darkness, keeping all night-owls, even those of an evil disposition, indoors. Sparrowhawk spent countless more solitary hours standing in snowdrifts, watching dancing flakes in the light of gas-lamps, or peering at the winter constellations far overhead with only the dense vapour of his breath to disturb the stillness. No-one else came to Doughty Street. As the last night of his vigil approached, December 20th, he almost felt disappointed not to have seen the work through to the end. Miss Evangeline had told him that, from December 21st, others would take charge and he could stand down. It might be perverse of him but, though he'd been badly affected by certain events this month, he wondered if he'd be missing out in some way. That said, his disappointment was also tinged with excitement – for when his work was complete and he left Doughty Street for the last time, Miss Evangeline would surely reappear to officially conclude these strange proceedings.

In anticipation of this, he woke early on the afternoon of December 20th and, with two hours to spend before darkness fell, joined the crowd at Buckingham Palace, who were watching through the barred gates as Queen Victoria's so-called 'Christmas tree' was raised. The queen herself was in attendance, as was her new, famously dapper husband, Prince Albert of Saxe-Coburg.

Though both the royal couple were in their twenties, they were small, near-juvenile figures, almost invisible in their coats, scarfs and mufflers, and so surrounded were they by valets and

109

chamberlains. The queen, in particular, was extraordinarily short. Briefly, it seemed astonishing to Sparrowhawk that for so many lands and so many millions of people, this pleasant, petite little creature, now clapping her hands with girlish glee, was the official Head of State. Had she the first inkling, he wondered, of the power struggles and political machinations that were waged in her name, of the shady dealing and the bribery and the exploitation and the wars of devastation, not to mention the famine, desolation and misery that might result? Had she an inkling of the desolation and misery in her own capital city? It seemed unlikely she would think much on it even if she knew, but who could blame her? Who in the right mind would want to dwell on such things?

He switched his attention to the Christmas tree. It was a Norwegian spruce, about twelve feet tall and hung with apples and other kinds of fruit, and it took a good number of footmen to erect it. Sparrowhawk had heard of this curious custom before. Queen Charlotte, wife to King George III, had introduced it to the royal household from Germany, where apparently every moneyed family boasted one. He couldn't imagine that such an ostentatious celebration of Christmas would ever catch on widely in England, not least because, though the gathered crowd seemed fascinated by what they were witnessing, again there were at least as many waifs and strays among them who were less interested in spreading good will than in picking pockets and pinching young ladies' bottoms.

When Sparrowhawk finally went on duty that evening, he reflected on the week he'd just spent. One thing that had struck him while wandering the shopping streets and standing at the gates of the Palace – apart from the strange inconsistencies of the season – was the presence of so many couples, hand-in-hand, seemingly enjoying each other's presence more than usual. This started him thinking about Miss Evangeline again, and he remembered his last few words to her before he'd slept. Perhaps Christmas should be a more personal thing than a wild feast?

Maybe it would be a truly special time if one had someone special to share it with?

He hadn't seen her for several days by now, and he again wondered why.

While it wouldn't be true to say that his desire for her had dwindled, it had perhaps steadied. He was an adult, he kept reminding himself, not an adolescent. And adults understood that you couldn't always have what you wanted. She had lain with him, it was true, but only on one occasion and maybe for a purpose. She'd seemed saddened by what she'd done, and not just for herself. None of those signs promised much. At the time he'd convinced himself that he could win her over, that she had to – that deep down she *must* – feel the same way as he. Hadn't she kissed him with fervour? Hadn't they rolled together willingly, their sweat-slick bodies sliding in perfect unison?

Such ruminations kept him frustrated, but they also kept him awake – which was a good thing. Had his guard been down at around two o'clock in the morning, he would never have noticed the moving blob of eerie, silver light. It was so pale, so ethereal that it may not even have been noticeable outside in this world of snow, ice and drifting, spectral mist. But it was clearly noticeable *inside*.

Sparrowhawk came quickly alert.

It was inside the house – inside number 48.

He watched it move behind the curtain of each downtairs window like an archetypical ghost, apparently heedless of any dividing walls or doors. Bewildered and alarmed, he scrambled through the rhododendrons and over the park railings, and ran across the road. The front door to the house was closed and locked; its windows were secured. Nobody had entered this way. It occurred to him that a servant might have risen from their bed, possibly to complete some late night chore. But he soon dismissed that. Once lights had been extinguished at number 48, he'd never seen any movement until morning.

He circled swiftly around to the rear. In the alley, the snow lay deep and crisp, but had been broken many times by the passage of pedestrians earlier that evening. It was impossible to tell if anyone had been here recently. The dustbin lids told no tale either, as they had been frozen in place at least a week ago. Hooking his elbows over the wall, he raised himself up and, thanks to the moonlit snow in the garden, could visualise the entire property.

One of its rear downstairs windows had been jammed half way open.

While Sparrowhawk had been idling the shift away, pondering problems of the heart, a third party had forced entry.

In a single, liquid movement, which he'd have been incapable of on the day of his release from the Fleet, he swung his body up and over the wall, and hurried across the lawn. He infiltrated the building through the same opening the intruder had, and found himself in a small scullery. Moving forwards, he was struck in the face by something cold, yielding and covered in hard feathers. He jumped back, drawing his shotgun – but his eyes were now attuning to the 'snow light' from outside, and he saw three hanging fowl: a pheasant, a partridge and a goose, probably destined for the Christmas table. Cursing quietly, he stepped around them, opened the scullery door and moved into what he assumed was a kitchen. Pots and pants glinted on shelves, while cutlery and crockery was arrayed on a central table. Now, he saw the light again – glimmering around a half-open door.

He went stealthily through this and down three steps into a washroom that was so narrow and bare it was more like a brick passage. At its far end, a figure stood with back turned. She was female – that was clear from the curves beneath her diaphonous nightgown and the chestnut braids falling to the small of her back.

Sparrowhawk was alarmed. He wondered if his first assumption was correct, and that he'd stumbled upon a servant engaged in late chores, or, worse still, the mistress of the house. Yet – the strange, silvery light filled this place, and he couldn't see where it emanated from. There was no lamp or candle. His hair stiffened as it dawned on him that its source might be the woman herself.

"Hello," she said, without looking around. "I've been expecting you."

He ventured forwards, shotgun levelled. "You ..." He could barely speak, his mouth was suddenly so dry. "You ... you've been expecting *me?*"

"Of course."

She turned to face him. Sparrowhawk's jaw dropped almost to his chest.

"M-my God," he stuttered. "My God ... *Leticia!*"

XIV

Leticia was 'peaches and cream' pretty, as she'd always been: her lips strawberry pink, her eyes peppermint green; soft freckles dusted her nose. When she saw the shotgun, she pouted.

"Will you kill me again, my husband?"

"Leticia ... don't say that. You know, you know I didn't ... "

She smiled mischievously, and lifted the hem of her gown, revealing first her smooth, milk-pale thighs, and then the naked cleft of her 'peach', as she'd used to call it – moist and razored clean, only one of several wanton acts she'd performed towards the end of their relationship to try and win him back to her bed.

"Will you stick that big gun of yours into my nether-parts?" she wondered. "Will you blow asunder those useless organs that doomed our marriage?"

"No, Leticia pleeease ..."

"No?" She looked shocked, but continued to flaunt herself, holding her gown to her navel. "You wanted me the first time I did this. And the second. And the third, as I recall ..."

"Leticia, stop this!" He shook his head, too shocked to even think clearly. "Those were momentary lusts ... momentary lusts that meant nothing."

"Nothing?" She looked hurt. Her gown rustled to the floor.

"I'm ashamed of them, if that's what you want to hear. You were my wife. I had the right to bed you, but I regret it ..."

"You regret my impregnation with our second child?"

"Of course, given how it ended."

She looked disappointed. "John Sparrowhawk, you are as poor a liar now as you were when we were married. You don't regret it... for ultimately it freed you."

Despite all, this left him incredulous. "You think I wanted you to die?"

"You'd never have abandoned me. You were too much an officer and a gentleman for that. So, the answer to your question must be ... 'yes'."

"Leticia, enough of this! You … you can't be here!"

"Oh, but I can. And I am." Her laugher tinkled like broken glass. She plucked fetchingly at her chestnut curls. "I *must* be, John, for I'm never away from this Limbo of ice and mist."

She indicated the room around them, and only now did he notice the extent to which the cold had permeated the house. The paved floor and brick walls gleamed with frost; a line of icicles hung from a crack in the ceiling. Sparrowhawk's breath puffed in clouds of vapour, though Leticia's breath, he noticed, didn't puff at all. Silently, she glided past him and ascended the steps. He followed, and saw that the silvery light now filled the kitchen, as did the ice – every nook and cranny was covered with a blueish glaze. And yet the room was clearly recognisable to him. He was no longer in Bloomsbury. This was their own kitchen in Little Chelsea – not just in dimension, but in fittings. The pink tea caddy that his in-laws had bought them as a grudging wedding present sat on the hob. On one of the shelves was the engraved silver tankard that his platoon had presented him with on his promotion to captain.

Leticia turned to face him. She smiled again, but it was a wintry smile. "This is my lot, John. My eternity. But it consoles me that I earned it in your service."

"My service? I … I don't understand."

"You wanted me to die, and I wanted you to be happy. So this is the price I paid."

"What are you talking about?"

Her smile faded. The green eyes lost their lustre and receded into their sockets; her teeth became prominent, skeletal. "You know why my parents never revealed my resting place to you, John? Because suicides can only be buried in unmarked graves."

"Suicides?" The word struck him like a hammer blow. "But Leticia, you're no …"

His words petered out. Could she have? Was it possible? It was almost too horrible to contemplate, but suddenly the likelihood seemed immense. Had he – *good Lord, no!* – had he driven the poor child to such a brink of despair? His eyes filled with tears, which immediately crystalised in his lashes.

"Oh, don't fret, my love," she said. "It wasn't so bad. What are a few extra drams of medicine to an ailing, sickly girl?"

"Letcicia, you did not take your own life! Please tell me you didn't!"

"Why not? This place is a measure of the worthlessness of that life."

They were now moving around the downstairs of the house. Only Leticia's unearthly radiance lit the way. He saw endless familiar features. The maroon wallpaper with the white polka dots, which Leticia hadn't liked but which he had insisted on buying, and which now clad the entire ground floor – where it had sagged into a million damp, frozen crinkles. In a corner of the drawing room, Leticia's piano stood laden with snow, as though it had only just been brought in from outside. Over the hearth hung the oil painting of themselves they'd commissioned after their wedding; it depicted a young couple whose demeanour was chillier than it should have been. Appropriately, it now dangled with icicles.

Leticia glided through it all this decayed memorabilia painlessly, though her naked feet were black with frostbite.

"Leticia!" he pleaded as he followed. "Leticia, you were tortured by grief and despair, but not … not to this extent. Please tell me you weren't."

She eyed him wearily, as if unable to believe that in the midst of all this suffering he again had thoughts only for himself.

"Look, I was a coward," he said. "I ran from my responsibilities. I know that now. But you could not … you weren't so distraught that you … please say you didn't!"

"None of it matters any more, John." Her tone was placating. "Come, let us go upstairs."

"Upstairs … why?"

"For old time's sake, perhaps?" She started up, but he hesitated.

116

"Leticia, wait."

She stopped, turned.

"Leticia, you need to … look, what I did to you was unspeakable. Never a night has passed when I didn't regret it. But only when I came home did they tell me you were dead … they withheld it from me while I was in Afghanistan. Firstly because I was beyond the reach of messages, and later because I was wounded. By all accounts, they feared the news would complete the job the Afghans began. But then I came home and found this house empty … I went temporarily insane. I drank, I gambled, I spent every penny we had left. But that was for you, Leticia. After Afghanistan, I so wanted to see you again …"

She continued her ascent. "And still you lie, John Sparrowhawk."

"Leticia wait!" He followed her upstairs. "It's not a lie! I wanted you!"

"You wanted a nurse." She was part way along the upper landing when she again turned to face him. "Someone whose shoulder you could cry on after your dreadful ordeal. But how did your ordeal compare to mine? Did you consider that?" Her own eyes were now tearful. "I'd have been delighted to nurse you, John … had I thought it would lead to better things. But I knew that it wouldn't … that my tender and loving care would be as useful to you as my peach. Something merely for the moment."

"Leticia …"

"Your ordeal would have ended, but mine would have gone on. And indeed, it still does. As you can see."

"Leticia, I can only say I'm sorry so many times."

"But when will you mean it, dear John?"

"Right now. Let me prove that to you. Tell me where they buried you."

She pondered this, shuddering. "One crossroads is much like another."

"Tell me, please. So I can reclaim you and bury you properly."

"But … you can *never* reclaim me, John." She seemed surprised that he didn't realise this. "Not even you, the hero of Kabul."

"Who says I can't?"

"Why, the master of this realm."

"What … ?"

"Oh, my dear husband … I'm beyond your reach. I lie with another. Even now, he awaits my comforts."

She pushed open a door, and on the other side was their old bedroom. The unnatural cold had penetrated even into this homely place. Filigrees of ice clung to the hangings over the bed. The carpet crunched with frost. But none of these drew his attention as much as the mop of dark hair on the pillow.

"Who is that?" Sparrowhawk said.

"One who sleeps in this bed whenever he wishes. And who ravishes its occupant at a whim."

He glanced round at her: she was full and beautiful again, her corpse-like pallor replaced by a rosy, lustful glow.

"That's right, John, he ravishes me – whenever it suits him. And I let him. And do you know why I let him? Because ravishment is the only form of love I've ever known."

"He hurts you?" Sparrowhawk whispered.

"Not physically." She pursed her bright, pink lips. "I've never been hurt physically."

"But he takes you against your will?"

"I have no will. I never have had since the day I met him."

Sparrowhawk felt the muscles bunch in his neck as he surveyed the rest of the room. He knew every inch of it. Above the dresser, there was a small oval painting of his mother, looking fey and beautiful when she was young – it was the only thing he'd inherited from her when she'd died. It now hung skew-wiff, its frame fringed with tendrils of ice. But his mother's eyes were on him, fixedly, as they had been since the day he'd first seduced Leticia.

He tried to look away, but it was impossible. His well of self-loathing reached uncontrollable mass, and the rage spewed forth. With a roar, he spun around, brought the Greener to his shoulder and jammed its muzzle against the head of the sleeping man. Reaching down, he yanked back the quilt. The man remained asleep. He was half-smiling, as if to say: "Nothing, not even a sawn-off shotgun, will disturb *me* when I want rest". It was an attitude as familiar as the face, for Sparrowhawk found himself peering down the barrels at someone who could only be his twin brother. The sleeper's hair was thicker, his sideburns sharper, his features slightly chubbier – but in all other aspects the two of them were identical.

Leticia's response was to giggle, then to cover her mouth coquettishly. "What were you expecting? A gargoyle?"

"That … that is not me," Sparrowhawk said in a strangled voice.

She mused. "There are some differences. Time and bitter experience will do that to a man. You're not quite as sneery now. Certainly not as arrogant. But in truth, these variations are negligible."

Globules of sweat stood on Sparrowhawk's brow, but he continued to aim his weapon. "You expect me to destroy myself? Is that it? As a final sacrifice?"

"I fear you lack the courage for that?"

"It's not about courage. Leticia, I'd do anything to take this pain away from us. But is it achievable? If I do this, will you be released?"

"Who knows?" She breezed around the bed towards him, her hands joined. "Who knows what an act of true love, however belated, may accomplish."

Sparrowhawk cocked both barrels. The sleeper slept on, smiling in his deep and secret way. But now something in the detachment of this man, something in his immovability, his impartiality to the woes of those around him, made Sparrowhawk think twice. This was too simple an answer. It had always been too simple for Sparrowhawk to pull a trigger – even on himself, for what kind of solution would that provide? And now, slowly and surely, a terrible understanding dawned on him.

119

He shook his head, at first imperceptibly but then more vigorously.

"Leticia … I can't perform an act of true love for you. Not now, not ever."

"John!" She sounded hurt again. "John, I beseech you!"

"Beseech me not!" He glanced round at her. "It's beyond my power. For I never loved you before. And now it's even worse … now I love someone else."

"Someone else?" For the first time, his dead wife looked surprised.

"You must endure whatever judgement has been passed on you," he said.

"John, you can save me …"

"With yet another lie? Of course I can't!"

"You love someone else?" Sowly, her expression of surprise gave way to one of peevish resentment. "You, who rotted in prison as a rake and gambler, without a friend in the world, without a relative who'll acknowledge you? How can you love someone else? How can they possibly love you?"

"How indeed?" he said, reassessing Miss Evangeline's promise to 'gird him for the fight', and at last realising why she had given herself to him.

"You will be punished for this!" Leticia hissed.

"You have no idea how much," Sparrowhawk said, his heart sinking like a stone.

Leticia hissed again, but he barely heard her. She was no longer a sensual beauty, but a corpse with sunken flesh, peg teeth and empty sockets for eyes; her diaphonous nightgown was in fact her shroud. But he saw none of this. He didn't even look at her as, slashing and clawing like a deranged cat, she dwindled at speed along a cylindrical tunnel down which a million snowflakes billowed. Wind blasted him with a sword's edge, and wailed shrilly in his ears. It almost knocked him from his feet, but he stood against it, and when it finally settled he found that he was still in a bedroom – though not necessarily the same bedroom.

His shotgun was still in his hands, its muzzle still trained on the head of a sleeping man. But only with painful slowness did Sparrowhawk begin to realise who this man was, and exactly which room he was in.

He was warm, for the embers of a fire glowed in the grate; the room was carpeted, wood-panelled, hung with thick curtains. Was it possible this was the master bedoom at 48, Doughty Street? Confirmation lay on the pillow – the sleeper whose head he held his gun against was not some diabolic parody of himself, but the very fellow he'd been trusted to protect. Even now the man stirred; with one hand, he mussed his floppy brown hair. Alongside him, a woman – presumably his wife – also stirred.

Sparrowhawk held his breath as he hastily uncocked the weapon and glanced around. Morning light diffused between the drapes on the window. There came a muffled clip-clip of hooves from outside. Somewhere overhead, in the servants' quarters, there were rumbles of moving feet. Still holding his breath, he backed from the room, hurrying along the landing and down the darkened stair to the ground floor, praying that some of the domestics weren't already up and about.

His luck held – nobody was around, and the scullery window was still open. He climbed lithely out, drew the panel down behind him, and dashed across the garden. He vaulted the rear wall just as he sensed curtains being opened behind him.

He was still in a daze when he finally returned to Camden Town, though reality came like a dash of cold water when he entered his own bedroom and found a leather bolster and a large envelope on his bed.

He opened the bolster first, and was astonished to see it crammed with bundles of five-pound notes, all fastened together with string. When he tore the envelope open, three documents fell out. One was a letter written to him personally, and scented with rose and jasmine. The others were deeds of ownership – to Peppercorn, the horse that had served him so loyally despite the perishing temperatures it had been forced to withstand, and to the apartment in which he now resided; apparently it was his, either to live in or to sell as he saw fit.

He read the letter last:

Dear Captain Sparrowhawk

Please find a sum of ten thousand pounds in payment for the vigil you have successfully completed. Your horse and your home we bestow on you as Christmas gifts, but also in gratitude for the onerous work you accomlished against such difficult odds. We are sure you will also make good if you opt to sell those dreadful weapons of yours. Hopefully, you will never have need of them again.

It may also interest you, and we're sure will please you, to know that your late-wife, Leticia, died of natural causes and not by her own hand. She rests in the municipal cemetery off Caledonia Street, Pimlico, in a clearly marked grave.

John ... I apologise for the briefness of this note, and that I am not here in person to deliver it. I trust you will understand and forgive me in due course.

Your lasting friend
Evangeline

XV

Sparrowhawk had planned to rest long into the day on completion of the vigil, but he slept poorly that morning, his confused dreams filled with relief but also with bitter resentment. He finally rose at two o'clock in the afternoon, took Peppercorn from the stable and headed for Pimlico. The cemetery was close to the Thames, at which reach people were actually daring to skate – something Sparrowhawk had heard about in times past but had never witnessed. He found Leticia's grave easily, as the letter had said he would, and brushed snowflakes away from its carved eulogy, which read:

A beloved daughter
Deeply missed

There was no mention that she had also been a wife and mother. He placed a wreathe of holly on the grave and said an awkard prayer or two, before leaving the cemetery and steering his mount across the city towards Bloomsbury. He arrived at Doughty Street just as the man he'd been guarding at number 48 emerged from the house, pulling on his gloves and greatcoat. His topper was perched at a precarious angle, and he had another great wad of papers tucked under his arm. He leapt into his carriage and was driven away at speed.

Sparrowhawk had to canter through the evening traffic to keep up. Unsurprisingly, the trail led to Piccadilly. The carriage dropped the gentleman off at the alley he had visited before, and he walked quickly up it, leafing through his pages as he went, finally disappearing through the same tradesman's door. Sparrowhawk rode up to it, just as a young fellow, who, by the black stains on his hands, face and bottle-green apron, was a printworker, was about to close the door.

"May I help you, sir?" the young fellow asked, surprised to see a tall, taciturn horseman towering over him.

123

"What is this place?" Sparrowhawk said.

"This place, sir? Why this is *Chapman & Hall*."

"And who, pray, are Chapman and Hall?"

The young fellow seemed a little put out by the question, which he clearly felt was a slight on his masters. "Chapman and Hall, the publishers, sir."

"Publishers?"

"That's right, sir."

"Pamphlets and the like? Legal documents?"

"All sorts, sir."

"I see." Sparrowhawk felt a growing sense of angry bewilderment. "And are they engaged in some kind of government work, at present?"

The young fellow thought about this. "Not as I'm aware, sir."

"Would you tell me if they were?"

"I'm sorry, sir?"

"Who … tell me this, young fella. *Who* is that gentleman who has just gone inside?"

"Just now, sir?"

"That's correct."

"Why, that's Mr. Dickens, sir. Did you not recognise him?"

"Mr. Dickens?"

"Mr. Charles Dickens."

"The journalist chap?"

"Well, he has some reputation as a journalist, sir, there's no denying it. But I think he's better known these days as a book writer."

"A book writer!" Sparrowhawk almost spat the words.

"That's right, sir. And he's just delivered to us the final chapters of his latest masterpiece. It's to be called *A Christmas Carol*, and thankfully it'll now be ready for purchase in time for Christmas Eve. It's a marvelous tale, about …"

"I don't want to know what it's about!" Sparrowhawk roared. "Why the devil should I want to know that?"

The young fellow clamped his mouth shut. He looked

thoroughly abashed.

"You tell Mr. Charles Dickens, you tell him … that …"

Unable to articulate how he felt, Sparrowhawk wheeled his horse around – no mean feat in the narrow passage – and galloped back towards the lights and noise of Piccadilly. Of course, it would serve no purpose careering around the centre of Westminster, no matter how perplexed and infuriated he was, so at length, in the knowledge that his vigil was complete and that none of London's byways were closed to him any more, he eventually turned his horse in the direction of Eastcheap.

It was only a half-hour ride away, but when he got there the winter dusk was falling. He found Rislington Row quickly. It was a side road passing between open patches of frozen wasteland. There had once been many buildings here, but all had now been demolished – except one, which stood right at the end and bore the flaking numeral *13* on its gatepost. Sparrowhawk gazed up at it.

It was a church, or what remained of one.

In truth, it was more like a hollow shell. Its roof had gone, and where once there'd been stained glass windows now there were empty apertures. Its main door hung from its hinges, creating a gap through which one could enter. He dismounted, but before going inside, he heard the faint, harmonious strains of *Silent Night*.

He glanced behind him and, some distance over the white-clad roofs of the business district, he spied the majestic dome of St. Paul's Cathedral. A ruddy light emanated from its lower windows. The choralists were inside, probably practising for the Christmas Eve service in three days' time. There must have been a great number of them to make themselves heard over this distance, and for a brief moment in that cold, brittle night it was the most beautiful sound he'd ever heard. It soothed him somewhat as he turned and entered the church. According to an inscription over the lintel, it had once had been devoted to Saint Sebastian, who, if Sparrowhawk's classroom memories were not too fogged, was the patron saint of soldiers.

Inside, there was nothing of consequence. Instead of lines of pews, he found tangles of dead thorns; the door to the sacristy led only to snow-covered rubble. He mooched around a little, but feeling helpless and strangely vulnerable, he finally turned to leave – but before he could, he spotted an alcove near the church's main door containing a heavy piece of statuary.

He made his way over to it.

A marble font, filled with ice, was clasped in the hands of a life-size marble angel. Both objects were scabrous with age, riddled with fissures. The angel, who, by her shapely form, was intended to be female, had suffered the most. Her face was black and had crumbled to the point where it was unrecognisable – though, just fleetingly, Sparrowhawk fancied there was something familiar in it. He shook his head, baffled by the illusion. In the cathedral meanwhile, the choir had switched to another carol:

God rest you merry Gentlemen,
Let nothing you dismay;
Remember Christ our Saviour,
Was born on Christmas-day;

Sparrowhawk had never really known Christmas, but this was a carol that he particularly liked, with its message of hope in the face of extreme peril. He moved to to the doorway, but then glanced back at the faceless angel.

To save our souls from Satan's power,
Which had long time gone astray …

He wonded if the marble pendant she wore at her throat might match any other pendants he'd had contact with recently. He also wondered if it was his imagination that he'd caught the faintest scent from her of rose and jasmine. It would be easy enough to go back over there and check. But why should he? He was still too angry for it to matter, too angry to be awed by any of these events – and that, he supposed, was the way he should keep

126

it. Anger was a good emotion in that respect; it helped suppress those other, less useful ones.

He left the church and walked along the snowy road, to where Peppercorn was pulling at a tuft of weeds. Again, the loyal animal nuzzled him, blowing steamy breath all over him. It reminded Sparrowhawk that he was back in the real world, which was all he needed concern himself with. He must bank his earnings, he decided. And then he must make good his ownership of the property in Camden Town. After that, Kirkham in Lancashire. It was a long, icy road that he faced, but, with best foot forwards, he might still make it for Christmas Eve.

The End

About the Author

Paul Finch is a former cop and journalist, now full-time writer. Having written for the television series *The Bill* plus children's animation and *Dr Who* audio dramas, he is best known for his horror fiction, with 10 books and over 300 stories published on both sides of the Atlantic.

His most recent book is *Stronghold* from Abaddon Books, and the no-hold's-barred crime novel *The Nice Guys' Club* is forthcoming.

He has won the British Fantasy Award twice (Best Collection and Novella) plus an International Horror Guild Award.

Paul lives in Wigan, Lancashire with his wife Cathy and his children, Eleanor and Harry.